ACKNOWLEDGMENTS

Thanks to my friends and supporters in SnoValley Writes! and FreeValley Publishing. Additional gratitude to Casondra Brewster for everything, Victoria Bastedo, T.A. Henry, and Kathleen Gabriel for indispensable beta reads, and dedmanshootn, Rachel Barnard, Sarah Salter and David S. Moore for ARC comments that ignited my fire, kept my feet on the ground and saved me from silly misses.

Cheers to Pioneer Coffee NB and The Black Dog Arts Café.
I love you all!

= ONE =

Emmaline slogged along after departing the bus. The ubiquitous Seattle November rain oozed into her worn boots as the leaden grey of the sky seeped into her soul. "Damn," breathed out of her with so little energy it didn't even raise the brow of the Anne-Klein-wearing, wanna-be that passed her by. 'Anne's' boots were so platformed she would never feel the rain.

A splash of magenta on yellow pulled Emmaline's chin up from its morning funk. Mendlon's Gallery. An oasis of color in the desert of the city's cement and muck. Her eyes drank it in as she passed. The chill of her soggy sock retreated from consciousness as she drifted back into the creative daze of last night's inspired bout of painting. A sidewalk crack brought her tripping back to reality.

"Damn!" This time she made an impression on the gentlemen she was coming up behind. They glanced back, and she reddened when she realized one was the VP of sales. She hiked up her heavy shoulder pack and tucked her chin again. Maybe he wouldn't recognize her in her brimmed Gore-Tex hat and street boots. That's one good thing the business monkey suit provided - anonymity on the outside. Inside corporate world, everyone looked the same. Well, there were designer and basic monkeys, but within their work classes they were generic enough to blend. Her uniqueness was her own. Not to be shared with or soiled by the practical make-ends-meet crap.

A sudden luscious aroma stirred her as much as the richly mixed colors had. "Coffee," she whispered. Desire overwhelmed reason as she fished her last five out of her pocket.

"Double cappuccino, dry, please." She smiled at the sidewalk barista but didn't invite conversation. "Thanks, and I hope you stay dry," she tossed out along with a good tip.

He returned her smile. "Thank you and good day!" He gazed after her, but she didn't look back.

His sweet Italian features stayed in her mind's eye as she pushed forward. How many times had she bought coffee from him and never asked his name? She just labeled him barista-boy. Emmaline carried her precious drink untasted along the final block and glanced out at the snippet of the bay that peeked between the buildings near where she worked. A blast of rain in the face interrupted her appreciation of the last bit of nature she'd see until noon. At least the salt twang in the air was refreshing.

She whipped off her hat and bustled through the door of Schleagel-Martin Pharmaceuticals with a batch of noisy blondes. Gossiping already she supposed. She focused on guarding her espresso from unnecessary upset on her way through the frenzied lobby. She swore for the umpteenth time that she'd start arriving before the final horserace to desks-on-time. She coasted into the marketing department on the dot of nine.

"Good morning, Emmaleeeen," Arnie crooned as he came out of his private office.

Charlie snickered from his vantage point in their 'Batcave'. He was perched butt-on-desk, undoubtedly to see her dark hair bristle when the Crown Prince of Marketing mispronounced her name once again.

"Argh! Why does he have to do that every morning?" she puffed as she swung her pack under her desk and extracted her drenched coat from clinging to her body. She hung it on the rack by the door. "It's not funny!" she growled as Charlie scooted from desk to chair, noticeably trying not to smirk. His raised brows betrayed his amusement.

"Good morning, Emma-line," he exaggerated, drawing an invisible line from the beaming track lights to the height of her nose.

"Quit pointing at me," she grumped. Her intense grey eyes tipped up in her trademark eye roll. She smirked herself as she jimmied off her boots and switched to the 'girl shoes' she kept in her desk drawer.

"Rough night?" he asked while firing up her system for her. His was already in work mode displaying part of a new design in their corporate teal and red.

"No, fabulous, that's the whole problem. I was up till three. I finally broke through the block on the *Ancestral Island* piece and lost all track of time."

"Of reality, more like it," he teased.

"Exactly," she took the punch out of his line. "It's so much more real than being here. It's like I wake from a dream when I'm doing collage and paint, and everything is so clear and true. But then I feel like I wake up into life when I snap out of it too." She gracefully covered a yawn. "I just hope I can stay awake in one reality or the other." She sat at her desk and reverently took a long draw from her cappuccino cup. "Ahhh. At least there's *some* beauty in this Cracker Jack box."

"Hey, what about me? If this is a Cracker Jack box, then I must be the prize, right?" He tousled his brown curls and batted his remarkably long lashes over his smart chestnut eyes.

"Okay, wise guy. Let's just get to work."

They settled in, each in a world of their own. Charlie's fingers spun the workings of his mind through the keyboard onto the screen. A smooth rendering of ideas into reality. His skill bordered on virtuosity. Like Emmaline, he was driven to create, but without her philosophical chafing. Pharmaceutical logos, alternative band stickers, or a t-shirt for his nephew - it was all lines and forms, colors and textures, layers and effects. He just hated being interrupted. *Bleedahdiumph*. The infernal 'message in' chime frustrated his flow.

"Meeting at ten," Emmaline read in a voice full of gloom.

She saw Charlie's chin raise and lower like the old, rickety Fremont Bridge as he continued his creative trance without a care. Message received, she knew. And she also knew he trusted her to pull him out in time to get his game face on before the meeting.

3

Emmaline, on the other hand, lost all ability to focus. She sucked on her waning espresso. She opened the lid and scooped out the coffee-laced foam with her finger and set it on her tongue, unwilling to waste a single drop. Most people went for the easy latte, which they could guzzle through the lid without effort, but she considered cappuccino foam one of life's many hard-earned pleasures.

"Five minutes, Charlie," she announced perfectly to penetrate but not perturb his *wa*. She loved that term. She giggled inwardly as she remembered she learned it from an old video of *Shogun* - the miniseries. How embarrassing. She could have learned it in one of the Eastern philosophy books she read. She wished everyone was aware of the inner balance and focus of others. She wished even more they'd care a twit about leaving it undisturbed.

"Okay, Batgirl. It's time to leave the Batcave." Charlie grabbed his ribbed sweater and slung its Kelly green around his wide, lean shoulders with a half zip.

Emmaline jumped at his movement since she'd been expecting to rouse him instead. She liked his sweater, with the white band around one upper arm. How refreshing the designer resisted the urge to ring both arms in bland symmetry.

"Any idea what this mess is to be about?" He piped.

"Shh," she cautioned as she swung their office door wide. "Not sure, but Arnie called it." Her eyes gave him a silver flash of resignation.

She led the way into the meeting room, grabbing a cup of ice water and foregoing the ever-present donuts. She placed herself at the far end of the smoked-glass table where she could doodle on the agenda without catching too much flack. Squirming into the black leather chair, she moved forward to rest her dangling feet somewhat on the floor. It sucked to be short.

Charlie sat on a chair far from the table and crossed one ankle over its opposite knee, leg akimbo. There was something bird-like in the pose. But he didn't have the keen gaze of a bird. One couldn't tell whether his mind was on the speaker or something else entirely.

Arnie's epiglottis bobbed on his too visible throat as he yammered the introduction and continued to mouth-breathe. If he just didn't have to be so gung ho. Every idea was the best one ever. At least he was a non-partisan cheerleader. She could almost like him if he just wasn't so repugnant. And dumb. She scolded herself for being judgmental. Not everyone can be remarkably smart. There are some very dear and excellent people who can't add two and two. Her heart twanged for her grandfather whose wits had gone long before he left the earth. She tuned back in to the meeting. Joe from the Top office was speaking. She liked Joe's decisive demeanor.

"Product Development is going to give us a few words defining *Assimilaire* and its purpose. Benson." Joe held his hand out to the slight man whose brow was furrowed in determination.

"This is a product unlike any other. It interacts with the subject's brain chemistry to stimulate the same centers as those that respond when a person is at ease socially, such as at home with their loved ones or enjoying conversation with a good friend. Times when they feel as one with those around them. Many people lack social confidence or are incapacitated by a fear of groups. The extreme cases won't even leave their homes. *Assimilaire* offers them entrance into society and the potential to achieve their goals in cooperation with others rather than being held back by phobias. It offers the chance for fuller relationships. Their alienating differences are lost when they feel the same as others. It will be life-changing for many. People who have been plagued by the social anxiety of standing out won't even recognize themselves once *Assimilaire* comes to their rescue. They will fit in perfectly - one of the crowd."

Emmaline's mind wandered now that she understood the idea. She saw a gingerbread world with flat stamped-out people all in a line with piped-on sugar smiles. Joe's voice caught her attention again.

"So to sum up: what we need is to pull as a team, as Arnie has said, but in a new direction. Creating a pleasing face for the new release is not going to be enough. Branding will have to go beyond name and logo design this time. We need to take this one to the big time, and that means identity. A personality. We must create a relationship between the public and *Assimilaire*. Like it's a friend they'd like to know. A friend they'd like to keep close by their side. They must feel something in common with it. Believe it's just like they are. That it fits in where they live. A unified campaign. Got it?"

Nods all around.

"Okay, thanks for sitting through the presentation. Take the concepts with you and dream up a doozy! Remember it's all about ease, familiarity, comfort. This is an anti-anxiety pharmaceutical. Its whole purpose is to make you feel the same as others. We want the girl-next-door feeling. Dismissed." Joe stalked out the door with a direct example of back-to-work.

"Okay, team…" Arnie continued. But his thought was lost as the 'team' lost no time in hitting the showers. Lunch!

= TWO =

Emmaline bee-lined outside stopping just long enough to nab the tuna on rye and granny smith apple from her desk. She shoved her feet back into her boots and her arms into her coat sleeves as she reached the door. The air was crisp but warmed by the low golden sun. With pleasure she shed her coat and walked up the hill to the few lonely trees by the art museum. She puffed a bit as she crested the steep hill but her sudden intake of breath had nothing to do with exertion. The maples by the museum's steps were a mass of screaming scarlet-lemon-russet with an undertone of walnut-burgundy-maroon. She threw down her coat on the wide cement railing and sat enraptured as she swallowed her lunch without thought of its taste. Her face aimed at what seemed an impossibly pure cerulean sky.

Trained by her daily vocation Emmaline stood suddenly when done eating. She began shuffling back toward the Batcave as if a bell for return had wrung her heart out. She was still soaking in bits of fall's colorful bounty. Perhaps it could hold her through the rest of her corporate-grey workday.

=

She rustled her coat onto the rack and stuffed her boots under the desk taking her time in donning her girl shoes. Charlie was still in his computer world, though he'd switched from ear-buds and surfing back to design mode. He greeted her with a subconscious scratch of the springy curl rising from the cowlick at the crown of his skull. The oh-so-familiar gesture eased her into the afternoon's office-confinement with a little less angst.

"Girl-next-door feel. What the hell does that mean? This is a drug. Our ad campaigns for *Semiloth* and *Carinon* had nothing to do with creating relationship. It's usually about safe and efficient." She stared at the blinking cursor without inspiration. Her muttering rose into the ether. No reply from earth-to-Charlie. After a full five minutes without revelation, she decided on the direct approach. "Earth to Charlie," she announced in full radio voice.

Emmaline watched him emerge, his pace of full attention precise and predictable. Patience was a luxury she loved to afford him. She was amazed how many people labeled him a dolt because he wasn't instantly on their page. His pages were a lot more interesting than theirs if they'd take a quarter second to read them.

"What's up, Sunshine?" he twanged with a mellow grin.

"Trying to get my head around Joe's challenge. I'd love to bring in that doozy for him, but I've only got don'tzies. What the hell does he want from us?"

"Watch your mouth, Kinner. This is a place of business." Her lips performed a rosebud purse at his sarcastic use of her last name. "Eek!" he added just to rub in her despised initials. He raised his eyebrow in amusement and moved on. "Well, what did you glean from this morning's product presentation?"

"*Assimilaire's* a breakthrough anti-anxiety drug that works on one's brain chemistry to mimic psychological ease. Clinical trials report test subjects feeling tuned in to their surroundings and similar to those around them. Therefore they feel more accepted socially - like they belong. Nothing a good double martini can't accomplish if you ask me." She snorted lightly as she laughed.

"Ah, but there's where you're wrong. How I see it, the martini makes you oblivious to your surroundings and the differences between yourself and others. You feel you fit in because you're less aware of sticking out. If I'm reading this right…"

"And we all know you are, Genius…"

"…the beauty of this chemical is it tunes you in, not out, but you see the similarities between yourself and those around you. It helps you truly get along. You know, common ground. It's anti-alienation."

"Aha! I've got it, Charlie, we'll use Aliens! They fly in on their cigar shaped ships, which are now touted as IFO's - identified-with flying objects. The moment they land, they morph into the girl next door. All the way down the street it's nothing but friendly, sparkling-smile beauties in perfect harmony. The whole universe is content in oneness and understanding."

"Nice, Emmaline. You know I'm a sucker for aliens. Do you have a serious pitch?"

"It's an interesting concept. Comfort through sameness. Likeness. Is that what makes us like each other?"

"Hm, I don't know. You're one of the weirdest people I know, and I kinda like you, I suppose."

"Takes one to know one," she smiled. "I tend to like differences. But I guess even uniqueness can be a point of similarity if it's part of who you are and what you value. Another person's uniqueness would then give you common ground, as you call it, and make you the same. Now that you mention it, we're identical twins." No reaction from Charlie. "Seriously. I think we should contemplate what makes people like each other. Literally and affectionately. What is the draw of similarity? How can we demonstrate that?"

"Good thoughts. I knew you could do it Pahtnah," he drawled like a Western cowpoke.

"So what were you working on over there?" She swung her head at his workstation - now displaying a Hubble photos screensaver.

"I was playing with forms attempting to balance repetition and appeal. Likeness without dullness. If everyone was the same, do you think they'd be bored or happy?"

"Depends on if everyone was you or me!" She laughed a triumphant *ha* and flashed him shining eyes, brimming with glee.

He shared her glow and turned back to his design dilemma. Emmaline was well on track to puzzling through the pitch. Her thoughts turned inward, losing Charlie's being from her consciousness as surely as he would lose hers. Her mind had a long road to travel on this one. It went back to the Ancestral Island. The artwork had stirred her being. She felt the depth of Jung's description of this archetypal image. The idea that the experience and consciousness of all who came before was accessible and common to all. That this foundation could be tapped - like fossil fuel. The energy of everyone who had once lived, running through everyone living now. Providing understanding. Now that's likeness. Unity with infinite detail and variation. But if we all have the same roots, are we all the same? She wondered.

Charlie was buffeted by the clicking of keys as Emmaline let her stream of cosmic consciousness flow in a frenzied brainstorm. They'd be ready for tomorrow's First Reaction meeting. Arnie would be proud.

=

The two were interrupted as Jen came into their inner sanctum, marking five-o-one.

"Geez, five o'clock already?" Emmaline noticed.

Charlie and Jen exchanged a glance acknowledging the irony of her genuine shock. "And this is the girl who sees the nine-to-five as cruel and unusual punishment - in theory," Charlie quipped.

Jen waited while Emmaline stored her shoes and laced her boots.

"See ya, Charlie." Batgirl smiled.

"Yup, see ya for more fun and games tomorrow," he returned as he stuffed his iPod into his ears and exited the room.

"I don't know how you can work with him all day and not die of lust," Jen said as soon as he turned the corner.

"Oh, whatever Jen, you see every guy out there as gonads on wheels."

"No, really, there's just something about Charlie. I mean he's kind of geeky, but he's really built. Slim but strong. You know. And he's so - different."

"Yeah," Emmaline rolled her eyes and giggled. "You like him because he's not like you." She donned an evil smile.

"Yeah…Hey…whadda ya mean by that?"

"Come on, Jen. We're gonna be late for Life Drawing. I know you just like the nudity, but I really need to work on my line."

"I'm a serious artist too."

"Seriously horny."

"No, really. I draw trees and stuff as well as nudes. And Spencer says I have a unique vision."

"Yeah. Come on, Frost. Let's hit your road 'less traveled by.'"

"Okay," Jen said, unruffled. She really was an amiable sort.

= THREE =

Charlie walked the easy way tonight. Downhill toward Pioneer Square where he could take the gradual climb home to 12th. Plus that way he could kill some time at the bookstore before spending the evening with his leftover chili.

Designs kept turning in his head as The Stranglers blared in his ears. Funny how repetition of form brought ease and felt pleasing, but complete symmetry fell short of the mark for perfection. There needed to be some point of difference to hold the mind and give it that *ahh* factor. Except for designs that encompassed infinity - a figure eight, a perfect oval or circle. Somehow these worked. Designs that were evenly diminished like a spiral or graduated lines were satisfying too. The sameness seemed to go somewhere or mean something. One could identify with them - the way they fit together. His music changed to The Enigmas.

"Watch where you're going, Asshole!" a stylin' punk-in-his-own-mind shouted.

Charlie hadn't even brushed him. He must have entered his personal space. It must be part of the guy's get-up to be rude and aggressive, but he didn't even know what punk was. Designer ripped jeans and tons of studs, buckles and zippers. He was an obvious new millennium mimicker. In the 80's there was so much more. The Enigmas agreed - *Teenage Barnacle* - now that was a statement. Not just show.

At that time the attitude twists were more pointed and the extremists were for real, not bought at Macy's.

Although it could just be a matter of distance, he supposed. Time diminished familiarity and allowed one to sketch in the details. Whatever the case, retro independents fascinated him. He wished he could've been in Vancouver, B.C. back then, like his older sister - in the heart of the alternative, new wave, punk scene. He would give anything to have seen the Enigmas at The Railway Club. Too young. Too late. Now he was stuck surrounded by wanna-bes and copy-catters. It had all been done before. At least he could catch the fire of individual expression in the music. He had pirated his sister Sandi's collection and lived and breathed its contents. Vinyl to digital - now that's a conversion he could see as a miracle of God!

He eased through the door of the book store, taking a well-trodden path to Sci-Fi - drawn like a rocket scientist to atomic theory. He liked the hard stuff and expected the science to hold up to the latest research. But he wasn't opposed to the occasional otherworldly adventure, especially if it was psychologically complex and contained some great wit, like the Vorkosigan Saga. He'd worn out his copies with multiple readings. It'd be cool if someone wore out his custom designed t-shirts that way someday. Appreciated into oblivion.

Charlie picked up a book based on its awesome cover design. Three pages in - and nope, that one's a scrapper. He sifted through the stacks attracted by design and held only by good content. He stayed with nothing very long, though it was a long time before he left the store. He waved at Jessica, the unusual chick with red and black hair that always lurked behind the counter. She smiled, but he didn't stop to talk. His hollow stomach was hollering for food louder than The Sex Pistols were hollering in his ears.

He jimmied the lock with the key that supposedly fit the entrance to his apartment building. It probably would've been easier to bust down the wooden door, but he knew the drill and achieved it without wasted frustration. He took the steep narrow steps two at a time, oblivious to the odd old-building-smell. The odor subconsciously relaxed him—a well-known greeting that called out, 'home.'

Once inside, he docked his iPod in its state-of-the-art speaker box, dropped his shoulder pack and went straight for the microwave -

with a stop at the fridge. His homemade chili gave off a spicy, warm aroma that permeated the small studio.

He gathered his napkin, a tall glass of filtered water and parked his butt in a well-built, older office chair. He sat back like a captain at the helm and ate before his thirty inch monitor, sifting through a small selection of emails. He sent a quick reply accepting a date with a hiking buddy for Mount Si on Sunday.

At last he could go back to a collected list of links he'd been devouring. His latest interest was Incan patterns and the forms and lines that spoke of a whole society now lost. Only bits of their spoken language survived into modern times. Charlie found it fascinating that a culture so advanced in design and architecture didn't have a written language. It's as if pure design was enough. Even their social structure fit together with tight precision. From top to bottom it was formed from echoing blocks of hierarchical groups. From the imperious ruling family with its divine head to peasant groups of ten each ruled by a boss. They tended to use a lot of symmetry, but often with a different element or color to break the static feeling.

What he admired most was their stone work. How each stone was chosen for its fit and then carved down to bond with its neighbor. Each stone had an individual shape but there was complete unity and no gaps, even without mortar. The stone walls were so perfectly comprised that they had barely shifted or changed since they were built six hundred years ago. Charlie smiled. He loved how this blending of many individuals made a strong One.

As much as Charlie was drawn to the radical nature of '80's subculture, it was their wish for change - to create a culture for the individual - that appealed. He believed celebrating and utilizing differences would bring about harmony. That's why the ultra-consuming millennium punks sickened him. They took part in the material system and became copies of one another - and without cooperation. They were monotonous but also polarizing. They raged against the machine, but ran it with their own materialism. If people wanted less, and appreciated each other more, there'd be no need for disgusting politics at all. If he was an anarchist, there would be peace in his tiny world of one. If everyone was like him, there would be plenty for all.

The day's elections and their results passed him by unheeded as he put down his Murphy bed and grabbed one of the books from the stack on his nightstand. He read awhile and then smiled at the photo of his sister and nephew that sat at the foot of the lamp he was turning out. It was just another Tuesday. Another day in which he lived in the paradise of his mind, fueled by the hopes that inspired his designs.

=

Emmaline and Jen left the Life Drawing session after dark. Jen stretched the evening after class talking to and mooning over the coordinator, Spencer. While her friend schmoozed and flirted, Emmaline laid down gesso textures on boards. She wanted to try some new techniques. Not that 'new' was anything new for her. She lived to experiment - and was often rewarded with great results.

They endured their heavy packs with new energy now that the pages inside were filled with fresh creations. Emmaline was working on gesture and felt free and light after allowing her eye to command her with a wide flow of movement. The figures in her art had come to life in sweeping strokes and organic lines.

"Let's go to Two Bells and have that artichoke-garlic dip!" she cried out to Jen as they walked back into the heart of town.

"Ease up, Em, your exuberance is attracting the locals."

Emmaline mellowed her pace, sure that if Jen felt a red flag, it was time to take it easy. Walking at night with her was often an exercise in high security, with her low cut tops and short skirts. It was usually Jen chatting like a happy cartoon without a care. Emmaline was the protector. It just got away from her for a moment.

"Yeah, okay, but are you up for splitting a dip and grabbing a couple microbrews before we head back to Queen Anne?" she asked Jen in a subdued tone.

"Sure, I guess it's as cheap as anything else quick for dinner."

"Mine's going on the card anyway."

"Geez, girl. Don't get yourself in trouble."

"I won't. That's why I never have any cash though. I'll waste it all in a minute. If it's on a card, it's a bill, and I'll always pay it off. I just make sure I keep my limits much lower than my income warrants."

"I guess. If I carry a card I'm in over my head in five minutes," Jen admitted.

"Know thyself, my dear. That's the key."

The two entered the neighborhood tavern and chatted to each other, surrounded by the same folks as always. There were a couple free-for-alls in the discussions at the bar over the day's political turns. The girls swung their heads toward the abrupt shouts but didn't join in. It was all the same to Emmaline. To her, people would be people and the arguments between the parties would keep enough balance to stay her fears of true upheaval. No need to get involved. And Jen, well, she was just Jen. They enjoyed the comforting atmosphere of the well-known, until they rode the familiar bumpity 13 bus up the hill and parted ways to walk the rest of the way home.

= FOUR =

Emmaline hung her misted coat on the rack and decanted her feet from their boots. Her curly hair would be a mass of frizz when dry. It was a wild thing when the weather was 'mistifying'. She smiled. It was her favorite term to describe the never-ending drizzle of Seattle - invented one day when spouting about her 'do' as she came in to greet Charlie. Speaking of which, where was the Boy Wonder? She looked around and checked the time. Only two till. She dared to think he might be ill. It was so odd for him to arrive after her. Although it would be even stranger if he actually took a sick day. He was the old reliable. And she couldn't imagine him missing First Reaction. Worry set in all in a second.

The next second he wandered in. She was pulling on her girl shoes and missed his entrance. He tossed his shell at the rack and it crumpled to the floor. As she looked up, he took a long time bending and retrieving and placing it on the hook.

"Good God, Charlie, what happened to you? Did you take up drinking?" popped from her like a champagne cork.

"What, no 'good morning?'" he countered with his usual sarcasm, minus its usual zip.

She waited. He swung into his seat and settled back with a sigh. "No sleep," he explained. "Up all night thinking about the Incas. Thinking about this damned campaign."

"I know you're obsessive, Chuck, but you usually leave work at work. Even if you do work before workin' time and all the way through lunches." She used his scolding nickname. "And what the hell do the Incas have to do with it."

"I had these designs in my mind, and I kept finding the same idea in their repeated patterns. I think there's something to pattern and psychology of society - of belonging - of that feeling of fitting in. I think the repetition in design encourages group identity. But there has to be some interruption to symmetry for it to maintain attraction. I find it an amazing paradox that they used individually shaped and angled stone to build the most unified, solid walls in history. The individuals conform in purpose without being identical. The perfect design for our campaign. They belong together."

"So you stayed up so you could impress, Joe." Her tone was serious. It had the desired effect.

His dark-ringed eyes crinkled in a soft smile.

"It's a cool theory, Charlie, I can see why it kept you interested and took you off to dreamland without any shut-eye. Do you think the same repetition of pattern applies to crop circles?"

He didn't even twitch at the question since Emmaline would not pull his chain on such a thing. "Yeah, I took a look at some of those data too. And the pre-Inca Nasca culture that created the enormous line art on stone. Not sure where I'm going with it, but there's a pull, especially in repeated lines, that I think we could work with here. But it can't be too regular. I think there needs to be an individual element that becomes one with the whole."

"Okay, I'm game. I suppose you already did some mock-ups."

He held up his flash drive. "Not completely. I was just expanding the concept, but I've got some roughs saved that I can refine on time for the meeting after lunch."

"Surprise me. I want to see them when they're slick. But you've got me on a groove. I like the idea of the TV campaign having something repeated and then having something different added to catch interest. Making the odd element fit in well is the trick. Maybe conformists can be the boring repetition and a nerd can be the interesting twist that draws one in."

Charlie nodded his intrigue. "Sounds risky, but if you give the nerd - the odd one - enough depth and appeal it might work."

"Yeah, the plan is to have the unique one relate to the unity of what we identify with as an interesting group or sub-culture. Kind of a rootsy character. The many will be clone-like - static and lifeless."

"So the cool chick will outshine the blonde Barbies? I think you might be able to pull that off, Emmaline. Most marketing sets up fake perfection as a goal, but it leaves the viewer feeling alienated. They might buy the product subconsciously hoping to achieve perfection or feel closer to it for a moment, but they know it's an illusion. It leaves them empty. The big guy said he wants something different for this. Something with identity, like a friend. I think it makes sense to offer some integrity in the model. Girl next door is a deep, understanding, got-yer-back kind of woman that you can still fantasize about. Awesome. I'll leave it up to you to invent how to create that in a series of ads. But if anyone can do it, you can." He smiled, and she glimpsed his soul. Or maybe it was just that his eyes were so raw from lack of sleep.

She turned to her keyboard and began describing characteristics of this model she would recommend. She broke down the clichés, even the anti-model clichés like the Homer Simpson types. This wasn't about presenting a comfortable misfit; it was about presenting what it would be like to have something to fit in with - showing someone who felt good about themselves. They would need to exude confidence, but not empty pride. Talented. Wise. Caring. Strong in spirit. Individual but not strange. Someone like an artist, a writer. One who gained admiration through integrity of ideas and the work of their hands.

"Whew, this is going to be a tough casting," she mumbled as she looked back over her musings.

She continued and decided it would take more than one character to have this much character. It must be a woman and a man, but not in relationship with each other. While love was the ultimate 'belonging', that was far beyond the scope of a pharmaceutical, and she wouldn't even begin to take the image there. There was a longing to relate to others outside of love too, otherwise married couples wouldn't socialize. And she had met plenty of them who were neurotically anxious even with a supportive partner. So romance was out of the scene. But friendship between man and woman. That had an excellent balance. It fit with the Ancestral archetype. It felt 'right.' Plus it evoked a sense of higher or deeper consciousness. Security with the opposite sex. A novel concept to many people with anxiety disorders. Hell, with people in general. They saw each other as types, as models, as something defined - other than themselves. Like the others were manufactured bricks and they were natural stone. But stone is so much more real - appealing. That's it. Real. The model just needs to look like a real person. And in order to *look* real, they will have to *be* real.

"Hmm. Maybe it won't be so hard to cast after all. Anybody will do. Except anyone who shows up for a casting call - since they'll be acting." She smirked.

Charlie yawned a gaper, the back of his left wrist rising to his mouth on auto-pilot while his right hand continued to command the mouse to bring his exquisite design to perfection. Emmaline couldn't resist a peek.

"Whoa!"

Charlie jumped a mile at her loud burst of emotion.

"Sorry, Charlie. I just…"

"That's okay, my nerves are just edgy."

"No, my fault, I know better than to shout at you, but that's amazing. It makes me feel… I don't know…"

"At one with the universe?" he cracked in a mysterious voice.

"Well…yeah," she looked solemn.

He didn't take her awe lightly. "Thanks, Emmaline."

"I'm about done," he continued, "How goes it on the live ad front?"

"I think I've got the concept down. I just have to type out the proposal. It's going to be tricky to explain without them thinking I'm saying we should do nothing."

"Whadda ya mean? Are you channeling Seinfeld or something? No worries, you always have plenty of drama in your campaigns."

"But I want to use a real model. You know, a regular person, but not like Homer or something...more like...well, like us."

His lips pressed and then pursed, his eyebrows rising and falling in sync with them. "Interesting. Well, propose away. They can't say you didn't reach for something bigger. I'm not sure that's ever been done, not for a full-scale across-demographics product like a medication. You only see geeks and artists for niche products." He paused. "I think it's brilliant. Literally the girl next door. And it's one heck of a neighborhood." His evil grin returned.

Emmaline got lost in re-reading her work.

Charlie stood slowly. "Urgh," he groaned. "I gotta go get some water. Type," he commanded. He left her to her mad proposing and slunk out the door to the water cooler.

=

Charlie was accosted as he bent to fill his cup, by James from Marketing Logistics. He was one of the guys that brought their concepts and images to production. And he nearly bowled Charlie over with his hyper psychological pace on such a slow moving morning.

"Hey, Charlie, what're you guys brewing in there. Can I get a hint? I wanna get a jump on packaging design. Shiny, matte? Modern, retro, country comfort? What kind of thing are we talkin' here? Where are we going with this?"

"Morning, James." He emphasized 'morning' and drew the words out nice and slow, hoping against hope to communicate the hint. James squirmed as Charlie took a long pause to drink. Charlie would've found it funny if he wasn't so damn tired. "Nothing to report yet. First Reaction is this afternoon, remember?"

James' face fell and instantly jumped back to attack mode. "Can't you give me something? Just a clue? It really helps if I can get a feel for it. You know."

"Incas," Charlie dropped as the water hit his system and woke his urge to tease.

"Ink us?" James craned his neck like a thwarted ostrich.

"No, you know, like the lost civilization." He hid his amusement as he gulped the rest of the water and crushed his cup along with further chance for conversation. Charlie retreated to the Batcave with a purposeful stroll, and put his head down for a snooze. They were safe from interruption when the department was in think tank mode, and he knew Emmaline would wake him for lunch.

= FIVE =

Emmaline wandered the waterfront at noon. She picked up some fish and chips and sat on a bench overlooking the foggy netherworld of the bay. The sifting soft rain caressed her cheeks, enhancing her wistful mood. She loved this kind of November grey. The obscured water and shadowy islands suggested worlds beyond or left behind. There was a purity of being when the world was devoid of corners that were shown in sunlight's glare. One's spirit could travel beyond the surface, not sure of where matter ended and ideas began. And without fear of jagged points of reality. But her campaign was about defining Real. What made a person genuine? Someone you would trust. That you would want to be with. 'To have by your side,' as Joe had said. To her it was someone capable of these kinds of moments. Secure on their own. Who took time out to observe and store something - to later be able to give.

Her proposal was written, for better or worse. She realized she had described an ideal version of herself. A self-actualized Emmaline. But what did that woman look like? And part of why she was wistful - the man had turned out to be Charlie. Or some kind of grand Charlie, perhaps. Edgy and individual, but smart, wise, kind. Wit to make him interesting, quiet to make him approachable, athletic to show strength but with no sense of too much testosterone. Respectful. She was surprised she related that word to Charlie - the unquenchable tease. But he never hit below the belt with his humor. He told the truth. And his aim was always peace. He poked you and brought out your best. He created harmony somehow. That was the quality she wanted the campaign to show. Harmony.

They were working with a product that created a feeling of sameness with the goal of producing Harmony. But is conformity harmony? She thought it was key to harmony to have difference to begin with and then blend. Like a chord. Could a single note be harmonious?

The sharp cry of a seagull sliced through her. She popped her cell phone in and out of her coat pocket to check the time. Flipping the extra fries onto the ground, she carried her trash to the can. Emmaline blinked into the increasing rain as she looked toward the bay, watching gulls swing in to scoop up her fresh offering. Two ferries passed halfway out to Bainbridge Island, and she found herself gazing after the outbound boat.

"Back to work, Em," she told herself. "Time to see if the 'real' woman has a chance in corporate world. Another day, another dollar."

She came in to find Charlie looking alive, surfing pattern designs. "Are you sure you want to go with all Barbies and one cool chick?" he challenged. "I think it might be better to go with different cool chicks making an ultra-fine unit."

"Yeah, I came back a little early to rework my proposal. One note doesn't make harmony." She sat to change shoes, and her expression said talking was over until she worked it through.

At one-thirty sharp, Arnie came in to urge on the team. "Come on Emmaleen and Charles, we have an hour and a half to pitch our strategy to Joe before the rest of the big guys come down to see us hit it out of the park!" He scurried out with a strange loon-like giggle that was signature Arnie.

Emmaline shoved down her feelings of irritation at his slaughter of her name while she and Charlie followed on his heels. She thought about Arnie's uniqueness. He was different. He should be awesome then, right? Opposites attract. Attraction, not repulsion. "Must be we're polar opposites," she laughed to herself.

=

They sat around the cool, glass conference table to prepare for the three o'clock First Reaction presentation from Marketing to the Muckity-Mucks. Charlie had his trusty glass of water at his elbow. To his surprise, Emmaline selected a cinnamon sugar donut and was apparently planning to wash it down with a cup of what she called Corporate Combustible, the diesel-like coffee that ran the metabolism of men like Arnie. Charlie stood back up and filled another glass with water, setting it suggestively close to Emmaline's sphere of command at the table.

Charlie was glad he only had to say a few words at the meeting. His image would speak for itself. It was Emmaline who had to sell their concept. He was anxious for her, knowing the big guys were expecting something more conventional showing conformity. It might be tricky to convince them to go with the harmony angle or even to get them to grasp it. But the design was so much better than stiff symmetry. He'd spent the whole night making sure of it.

Everyone scooted up and played formal when Joe entered. "Good afternoon, team," the Marketing Head greeted.

All nodded, and Arnie replied, "Good afternoon, sir," as Joe settled in at his left, taking the place of honor.

"I trust you all have been contemplating the presentation yesterday and have formulated a strong First Reaction for me." He addressed Charlie and Emmaline with his eyes. "Charlie, let's project your branding images while Emmaline presents our conceptual choices."

Charlie plugged his flash drive into the presentation machine and pulled up his baby.

"Ooooo," was the summation of the group.

He took the cue to slide back into his seat and out of the dreaded limelight.

=

Emmaline stood next to the screen in front of them with way too much sugar, lard and acid-washed caffeine coursing through her system. Joe had said 'choices.' That had thrown her off her game. "Uh…"

"Wait a moment, please," Joe interrupted. "I just want to compliment Charlie on an extraordinary design. Great appeal. An excellent feeling of ease in it. Okay, Emmaline, shoot."

The moment hadn't helped her at all. Charlie was brilliant; she was what? Oh, On is what she was. "Um, the concept of unity and harmony is a complex one that's basic to our well-being. Those who are anxious in society most always feel they don't belong. Many blame this on their being different from others. If only they were the same, they would fit in, and everything would be perfect. Generally there's a belief that conformity or even uniformity is what brings unity."

They were all nodding, which was great, except this wasn't her point. She emboldened her resolve by remembering her musings on her actualized self.

"But being identical - matching a model - doesn't bring real satisfaction or harmony." She pushed through their puzzled looks. "Our angle is that Difference Unified is true harmony. One note repeated does not make a chord. It's different notes in accord that are music to your ears. Or to give a visual example - in keeping with Charlie's design - when you are yourself, in a niche you uniquely fill, you feel closest to those around you. When all of the stones are individual but fit with each other's odd shapes, it doesn't even take mortar to hold them together. Their whole is more unified, solid and lasting than any uniform molded-brick wall."

They weren't with her, but she had their rapt attention. They were willing to be convinced.

"Charlie's design is based on Incan stone work. Its beauty is in the exquisite fit of its varied shapes - so in tune with each other, they seem infinitely connected."

She saw lights going on.

"So although Development presented the product as making people feel the same as those around them and therefore accepted and at ease, we propose to spin it as a pleasing unity of uniqueness. Those different notes that create one beautiful chord. The static notion of identical psychological bricks to build a communal wall is instead spun as vibrant individually formed soul-stones that fit together like they were made for each other."

"Whew, okay, Emmaline," Joe broke in, "I think we have a clear grasp of the idea. Let's take a break before we hear the initial ad concepts that could rise from this. We need to decide if this twist flies. What do you think, Arnie?"

"It's way out, Emmaleen. You've really outdone yourself!" Diplomacy at its most cagey.

"But do you back it?" Joe cut to the point.

"Uh, I don't know that it's what Development was thinking."

"That's why they hired a marketing department," Emmaline jumped in before things got out of hand. "They want something big that creates relationship. Who relates to their own clone? You want friends who have intriguing features that meld with yours. You want someone next to you who supports your curves and imperfections, not an angular block with no give."

"Okay, you've got me interested enough to move on," Joe admitted. "Arnie? Anybody else?"

"I think it depends on how we're planning to illustrate it in a campaign," Lindsey, the new kid on the block, added without risk of contradiction. She leaned forward, elbows on the table and tented her hands before her perfectly painted lips, regarding Joe.

That would be a second on the moving-right-along in Emmaline's book. "So, what we imagined is illuminating difference by foregoing the typical models of the perfect society girl and guy. Rather than choosing Barbie and Adonis to present in our ads, we will literally present the girl and boy next door. Average, extraordinary people. Not anti-models like Homer Simpson, but confident nerds, artist types, people with depth and character. In First Reaction we think it's the out-of-the-ordinary Real model that's most attractive and comfortable to aspire to and identify with. Our anxious potential clients may see themselves in these people and better imagine they could be alongside them."

"Mmm. Flaw. Problem." Joe piped up. "Aren't these types thought of as outsiders?"

"Only outside of model perfection. Are the artificial, commercial actors the kind of people you would feel comfortable to be like and be with? Comparison to them makes one feel like an outsider. Would one feel at ease being In with them? What if, instead, they came into your world, and you became the most wonderful and comfortable you."

Nods all around. No one was protesting. Dead quiet.

"Okay. Seems you've put down direct opposition within the department. That means it's a keeper for final presentation today. And I think the visual is an absolute keeper," Joe decided. "What else have you got?"

"Um, that's it. Once we saw the depth of this, there was nothing else to consider."

"Whoa. No options? That's a tough sell, Emmaline."

"We gotta have options," Arnie the Prince-boy chimed in. "Of course your talent is thrilling, and your logic lovely. Very poetic. But what if they want more?"

"Does anyone have more to add? An off-shoot perhaps?" Joe hoped.

Emmaline liked to think the ensuing crickets signified nothing else stood up to the richness of their concept.

"Alright, then we'll present it with everything we've got. Let's talk about packaging options, and fleshing out the campaign." He turned to the statuesque red-head from Ad Production. "Marlene, please formulate what kind of unusual models you might like to cast. The big guns will be down in just over an hour to hear about the cohesive campaign."

Joe's voice trailed off in Emmaline's mind as her racing heart slowed in rhythm to her withdrawal into her seat. She took a huge gulp of her water. The corners of Charlie's mouth twitched back. Their 'rage against the machine' had a chance.

= SIX =

"Interesting perspective, Joe," Marcus Wananabe from the Top office spoke for the larger company. "Benson, how do you think that fits with the vision from Product Development?"

"It's kind of a stretch from the purpose of the product, I'd say. It's supposed to help people fit in, and although Marketing has presented a concept where people feel wanted, I just don't know if I'd see it in relation to a pharmaceutical. I think it might be more in keeping with the transformative nature of the product to bring the odd person out into the norm. We conceived of it as creating a feeling of normalcy."

Emmaline raised her hand, itching to pitch it in a way that Joe just didn't cover.

"We'll hear from you in a moment, Emmaline. We understand that you're part of the team that originated the idea, but I'd like to hear from Gerry with perspective on the image from Research and Development first," Marcus nodded to the older gentleman.

"Well, I think it makes sense to give it more of a hometown feel. Uh, I m'self wouldn't identify it was for me if there were a batch of plat'num blondes set up as the group for me to belong to. But maybe we still want 'em to be a bit prettier and more handsome than the common folk. This is s'posed to make your life better, right?" He spoke in his slow Virginia drawl as Emmaline twitched with impatience.

"Okay, Emmaline, what's your response?" Marcus led her.

"So what we're trying to get at is what is Better? There are plenty of lonely, lost, uncomfortable beautiful people. Most common folks think it's lonely at the top. So we bring it down a notch to Prettier than the Norm. What is Pretty? Does our consumer want to *look* happy or *be* happy? Development and the VP asked for a big campaign. We say let's show them how to *be* happy in the campaign. And to do this the characters in the ads must have depth. We need to define the characteristics that people aspire to. Yes, they want to Look appealing. We're not suggesting using people who look like the bottom of a shoe. We're suggesting something unique - yet universally sought after. We admire Confidence, Success. What breeds those? Talent, Intelligence, Knowledge, Integrity, Genuineness. We want models who exude a richness of being, who know themselves and are happy to be who they are."

To her shock, Charlie raised his hand to be acknowledged. She left off abruptly.

"Yes, Charles," Marcus said. Arnie squirmed.

"Um, I just wanted to, uh, reinforce the importance of the uniqueness of the models to work with the design I, uh, created for the product. The, the concept relies on each building block being varied in shape but perfectly fit into the whole. The design illustrates the concept that Joe and Emmaline have presented, and if it's decided the models should be more uniform, I'd like to withdraw this design and rework it for something more symmetrical. The harmony and strength of the design is in bringing together different shapes to make one. The many notes are necessary to strike the chord of strength and beauty. They all belong together."

Marcus hesitated, and seemed to contemplate. "Does that make sense to you, Benson and Gerry?"

Benson nodded, eyebrows up, mouth stretched down at the corners.

Gerry was silent, studying Charlie's design projection and then said, "Actually, yeah it does. It makes a lot o' sense. If this wall Charlie made was uniform bricks, it would be kinda' borin'. And if it had one different one, it would stick out a mile and ruin the appeal of the perfection. I can also see where if yeh brought the one different one into alignment to match the rest, it would give the feeling of forced uniform'ty instead of belongin'. And the Whole would be a rigid place to be, even if the odd one out did fit in now."

The corners of Charlie's mouth slid outward suppressing a wide smile. Emmaline glowed.

Benson spoke up, "After hearing more, I think this might fill the bill and be the big concept we hoped for. It's just more than we imagined for ourselves. I couldn't see it right away, but when you explain the visual design, I see how it mirrors the building blocks of personality transformation in the same way as we would like the product to be perceived. Its point was to bring people to a higher sense of social well-being, and this concept would show that in a way that's above and beyond any other marketing spin we've seen from anybody. There's been a move toward healthy, happy, fulfilled individuals in pharmaceutical ads, especially therapeutic medications like rheumatoid arthritis ads. But so far, they all seem to look rich. Mostly blonde. Usually older. And families or outdoor activities are the standard environment for them. If I'm hearing correctly, you're envisioning something different for these ads."

"Well, since we're in agreement that the concept may hold water, let's explore that further," Marcus moved. "What do you have in mind for actual scenarios, Joe?"

"Since this is First Reaction, I'm not sure we've spelled that out yet. Can you give us a general overview, Emmaline?" Joe gave her a make-it-happen glare.

"Um, what I envision is a series of ads featuring various young people entering social scenes that often produce discomfort. The character of our lead will appear noticeably different from the plastic scene around them. For instance, a young woman enters the judgmental club scene. The obvious would be to have her transform into the most beautiful woman in the place and join the poser crowd with copied appearance of ease. Instead, she will come in as an individual and hold her head high with confidence. She will go straight to the dance floor and dance her own moves. The dancers around her will conform to her style - admire her. The wall flowers that resemble a less vibrant version of her will come off the walls and join her to become the life of the party. The pretty plastic people who remain will fade back to become wall flowers."

"Hmm. Yes, I think we get the idea. Intriguing. Any comments?" Marcus opened the floor.

"I like the idea, and I can visualize the ad, but how are we going to make sure this unusual person is interesting enough for it to make sense when the others join her?" Barb from Sales asked.

"Emmaline?" Joe pointed with a nod.

"Well, we do have to use cliché images of some sort since this is a visual ad, not a novel. We'll use images of unique people that others admire. Artists, Writers, perhaps alternative athletes like Climbers. We want to stay away from elite images or classic model types. Remember the characteristics we mentioned earlier?"

"So we need to define what makes someone look talented?" Barb clarified.

"Exactly!" Emmaline enthused. "And intelligent, creative, noble - of great character."

"So let's brainstorm on what some of our characters could look like." Joe approached the white board. "Call out at will," he instructed.

"Maybe a unique hairstyle? Energetic, competent facial expression. Bookish. Creatively dressed."

"More specific on the dress," Joe coached.

"Loose tunic. Darker colors with lots of pattern. Asian influence to clothing cut. Soft leather. Designer, but uniquely styled not glam. Hiking gear."

"Okay. I heard 'bookish'. What does a writer look like?"

The room was silent.

"That one will probably have to be shown with context and props more than clothing," Emmaline admitted.

"What about the climber?" Joe suggested. "It would be easy to make him or her too elite. It's often an expensive hobby."

"We keep it more local." Charlie piped in. "My friends and I are climbers, but we're certainly not elite. I could lend the actor some gear if they're close to my size."

"Perhaps we can just hire you," Joe joked.

Charlie tipped his head with a crooked shy smile.

"That's a great idea," Barb blurted. "Charlie could be our climber and Emmaline could be our artist. They've already got the perfect character and wardrobe."

"Yeah, they've got the look." Benson seconded. He exchanged a nod with Marlene who handles casting.

"Uh, wait a minute," Emmaline protested, "that's a bit too literal."

"How so?" Joe fired back. "I think it's a great idea."

"But we're supposed to look confident and successful," she tried.

"You just succeeded in selling the concept for what promises to be a multi-million dollar ad campaign," Marcus pointed out, "and you did it without even having a back-up proposal. If that's not confident and successful, I'm not sure what is. And that's hard to find in combination with youth. We agreed we want to focus on a young, vibrant image as well."

"W-well…we're not actors." Charlie pointed out.

The room broke into spontaneous applause as the more weathered marketing veterans reveled in the prospect of leaving those temperamental casting call winners behind this time.

"If we understand you right," Joe pointed out, "those are just the kind of people you want to avoid. And it seems the rest of the crew do too." He laughed.

"What do you say, Marlene?" Marcus checked.

She cocked her refined brow and flipped her red tress behind her shoulder with a dramatic pause. "I love it!" she smiled.

"But what if we can't project for the camera?" Emmaline protested.

"That's what directors are for," Joe nodded to Jensen. "Do you think you can whip them into shape?"

"Sure," Jensen replied. "They're both colorful enough characters in their way. They have visual appeal. Fresh faces."

Emmaline crunched her fresh face into a disgruntled scowl. "But we're designers. We're background people."

"Welcome to the stage, Emmaline, front and center." Marcus announced decisively. "Unless in our last ten minutes you can come up with another campaign as breakthrough and strong as this one, I'm presenting this idea to the rest of the Top office. We're done with First Reaction. Let's break into our individual teams and continue to develop the idea at each level. If you come up with some sharpening details, please bring them to Joe who'll submit them to me before the end of the session.

The room began buzzing with the hum of one creative imagination merging with another, and the new concept caught the artistic fervor of each talent involved. While they built the conceptual equivalent of Charlie's Incan wall, Emmaline and Charlie fell back in their chairs and into their own private worlds - prone with fear and anxiety. The triumph they'd hoped for in convincing the others to celebrate the Real, fell prey to the knee-wobbling, sniveling of self-doubt.

= SEVEN =

Charlie and Emmaline inhabited their desks with absent, practiced motions. Shock got their tongues. Neither one picked up their mouse or pulled out their keyboard. Even Charlie was powerless to escape this one.

Emmaline finally broke into the terror of their thoughts. "They didn't assign us anything to work on this afternoon did they?" Her tone was dry.

"Nope." Charlie was no help.

"Maybe we should work on an alternate campaign. This was only First Reaction. Maybe the Top office won't buy it."

"Marcus loved it. We're in."

"You mean we're screwed," she slumped in her chair.

"How'd we end up in front of the cameras, Emmaline?"

She had to confess. "Well, to be honest, when I was out at lunch I realized the characters that fit the campaign's description were an ideal me...and an ideal you."

"You pitched us on purpose!?" She had never heard his voice so shrill.

"No of course not!" She calmed her wild tone. "I guess when I was reaching for Real, I found what I know best.

They're the ones that crowned us as confident and successful. I guess our ideal selves are the personalities they project on us."

"Are we there yet? Are we there yet?" he raised a brow and gave her a gloriously comforting snide smile.

"Just twenty-three more miles, dear," she flipped, in her best mommy imitation. She gave him a saccharine grin.

"Well we're gonna have to fake it quick. I hope Jensen's a good director."

"Yeah, he is," she assured without embracing the belief. "I've worked with him many times. Though never in front of the lens."

They both broke away into their own thoughts. The scuttling of their mice and madly clicking keyboards were the only signs of their fevered energy.

At five till five, Arnie came in. "Congratulations!" he said with stabbing-loud exuberance. "Not only did the Top office love it - you're Stars!! He grinned like a sugar-filled kindergartner waiting for answering joy. No joy. "You're to report to Jensen's area at nine a.m. tomorrow. Good luck!" His smile dropped at the corners as they only nodded. His expression lit to half a sunbeam as he tried, "Good night!"

"Good night, Arnie," they chimed in unison, then turned to each other and snickered.

They burst into giggles as the door shut on Arnie's now bubbling countenance. It took so little to light him up.

"And good riddance," Charlie stated.

"Yikes," Emmaline agreed. "He really doesn't have a clue does he?"

Charlie shook his head at a jaunty angle, and their eyes met in a grim moment of shared agony. "Stars," he mumbled.

"Yeah."

He got up and grabbed his rain shell. "Well, see you tomorrow, Your Worship."

"And you, oh Great One," she kowtowed in her chair as he disappeared.

Her smile faded as she stowed her girl shoes and laced her boots. Eyes were distant as she wrapped herself in her pea coat and shuffled out.

"Emmaline has left the building," she mumbled to herself.

=

Emmaline tromped up the hill and shoved her pack over to counterbalance as she leaned to unlock the security door. The carpeted steps squashed beneath her heavy spirit. She opened the double-locked door into her comfortable abode and set her pack just inside. Wiping her feet one more time on the welcome mat in the hall, she went for the couch. First line of business - boots off. They joined the wide assortment of other shoes under the end table next to her. She took a slug of water from the glass she'd left that morning and sighed as she wiggled her toes into some striped-socks that had been sticking out from her nearby oxfords.

"Star," she mumbled, wondering why she felt so depressed. Usually she came home on a high when they bought her newest campaign ideas. And her adventurous spirit would embrace almost any challenge. But being on stage was the worst. It brought out every insecurity she harbored. Sure she could pitch stuff in front of the marketing department, but that was just presenting a well-believed-in concept. The thought of being herself for the world to see brought her back to her attempt at poetry reading in public. Baring her soul under the spotlight left her a gasping, dizzy mess. The marketing team's praise of her as successful polished her confidence on the surface but her depths were a seething pile of poo. "I suck on stage!" she shouted at the silent pressure pushing her down into that inner mound of crap. "How did I end up here!?" And she wondered if Charlie felt the same.

Refusing to wallow in it, she got up and crossed the room to look out at the view. The sun had already set over the islands, but she could see the lights of the ferries crossing Elliot Bay and the twinkling lights of houses on the far shore. The sweep of the apartment and housing lights of Queen Anne dropped off from her window, down the hillside, to the inky expanse of water that was her sanity's haven on many an evening. Somehow that liquid reaching to the horizon allowed her soul to drift away from the hubbub of the city. Emmaline stood feeling it clear the bundle of dread that had knotted her into a frightened child. Turning back, she took comfort in the warm, vivid colors that embraced her from the paintings over the sofa. The bold strokes, alive with energy reminded her of the life that lay within her. She was an artist! If only the feeling would last.

She shuffled to the kitchen and rifled the fridge for something simple and comforting. It was breakfast-for-dinner night. Though she was functioning there was no energy left for serious cooking.

Emmaline balanced her egg and toast on their cobalt blue ceramic plate with a glass of OJ and her newly refilled water glass. She passed up the dining table and cozied onto the couch with her meal. She flipped on the tiny TV her dad had given her a couple years ago. Emmaline didn't own a larger one so she wouldn't be tempted to waste away in front of it. She swallowed her food without interest, took the dishes to the kitchen, swabbed them off, and planted herself back in front of a Seinfeld rerun. She had never seen this one.

She took up the cross-stitch she was trying to complete for a Christmas gift. Emmaline loved the tactile repetition of stitching by hand, and thrived on the tedious counting. She considered it slightly embarrassing that it was such a Square art form, but she grooved on watching the images emerge out of the complex rendering of color on the graph-like fabric. The more intricate the design the more she liked it, and it didn't matter if she stitched angels or elephants. It filled her fall and winter evenings alone. Bonus if someone else appreciated the finished product.

The old sitcoms strung together without notice, as she stitched her way into a blank consciousness, and got dozy enough to give her teeth a quick brushing and fall into bed. She pulled her grandma-made quilt around her ears without enough energy left to fret about tomorrow.

=

Charlie took the bookstore route home again. This time spending less time rejecting poorly written tripe and more time talking to

Jessica. He was bolstered by her responsive baby-blues as they talked shop. She was a sci-fi-head too, and retained more than the latest space battle or devastating alien. He loved to banter over the latest in scientific and techno speculation with someone more well-read than himself. And it didn't hurt that she was his kind of sexy. On a day when he felt pushed out to walk the plank, it was a steadying force to engage her - at least in conversation.

Business picked up as the seven o'clock book-signing neared. He wasn't interested in the overly made-up romance author, but apparently someone was. He let Jessica do her job. She was at work after all. The thought of work sent a stab of nausea through him.

Out on the street, he wandered to the falafel place on Broadway. He didn't go out to eat often, but he just wasn't ready to go home. Their food passed muster on quality for him. Downright delicious, actually. The place was always packed.

He glanced sidelong at the line of street-kids that sat on the sidewalk and squeezed his way in at the back of the queue. The crowd created a sauna-like effect inside and he shed his shell down to his breathable black jean jacket. He ordered the jumbo, filled a glass of water from the tap tank and elbowed his way to a table - avoiding the more social counter seat. The cacophony was divine. He couldn't hear himself think.

He went easy on the hot sauce - not oblivious to tomorrow's obligations. Heart-burn was not on the agenda. He savored his meal, watching the local color that populated his urban home. Although his soul soared on the open side of a mountain, there was something in him that grooved on the variation of expression in the human animal. Especially when packed together, they seemed increasingly flamboyant. Some instinct flaring to keep their individuality from being swallowed up in the fray, perhaps. Or were they flaunting their colors to attract their own kind? Was intensity of style a cry for identification or individuation? Tomorrow he would be the poster child for conformity - because he was different. Emmaline had really done it this time!

Charlie crumpled the red and white checkered paper around the wrapper of his vanished falafel. He dropped it in the compostable can, recycled his paper cup, and deposited the red plastic basket on top as he slid by the line and back out the door.

He walked the streets for awhile until the characters disappeared and all that were left were riff-raff, ne'er-do-wells, drunks and outright criminals. He grappled with the sticky building door and let himself in for the night, resigned to whatever tomorrow would bring.

= EIGHT =

Thursday dawned to torrential downpours. Emmaline reveled in the sound of the rain hoping to drown her fear in the pleasure of the world's reflection of her misery. A dark day - it brightened her spirits. How bad could it be anyway?

As Emmaline entered the Batcave, she saw Charlie wiggling his toes into dry socks and shoes after his urban river-fording trek to work. She heard a sigh of appreciation escape him when the warmth caressed his tootsies.

"Mornin', Ms. Scarlet," he drawled. "Is there anathin' I kin getch yer wondaful self?"

"Aw huush," she played in return. "Y'all know I don't need anathin' 'til tea ta-am." She fanned herself with a manila folder and batted her eyes.

"Ready to hit the stage?" he grinned a shit-eater.

"Ugh. No! And you?"

"Not really, but here it goes."

"Yeah." She paused as she bent to stow her boots. "Maybe it won't be so bad. One day at a time. They're only gonna work out the script and storyboard with us today I would think. Unfortunately, since we're concept coordinators and stars, we're gonna to have to sit through the whole process.

They'll want our ideas on how our characters should appear. Maybe it would help if I do you and you do me."

"Interesting." He laughed and dove into his computer.

She was worried. He was up to something. She grabbed a notebook, opting for the tactile indulgence of pen-scratching, and began a character sketch of him:

A tall, brainy young man with an endearing cowlick enters the scene. He wears a burgundy fleece with a 'No Means No' and 'Bauhaus' patch on the left lapel over his heart. A traditional Himalayan woolen cap is pulled on as he walks across the parking lot from his car to join a group of generic looking climbers at the trailhead. They part in awe of his centered and balanced-looking strength. Their North Face standard gear looks plastic and plain compared to his unique style from his pom-pom hat down to his Army-issue retro boots. They begin the climb, and as he leads, they fall behind, changing from their plain, predictable gear to don unique color, seasoned boots, and ultimately his features. They fall in line catching up to his pace and admire him so much, they become him.

That ought to keep up with any bullshit he was creating about her. She smiled to herself, waiting for him to complete his shenanigans.

He turned his monitor. "Prepare for the reveal of the Mighty Emmaline, Artist Model of the Universe." He announced. He clicked open the file and watched her hand fly to her open mouth.

"Charlie!!" she exclaimed with his hoped-for outrage.

He morphed an old art group photo, that showed her in her pea coat and boots, into a picture of her standing with one arm in the air in a Nazi salute with a Hitler mustache. He replaced the other artists with a bowing group of minions - obviously copied from some kind of prayer ceremony. He changed their garb to the same black as her coat and added a copy of her wine-colored, billed beret to each of their bowed heads.

"Very funny," she twitched her mouth into a twisted grimace.

"Yeah, I thought so," he glowed back in amusement.

"Okay, well, listen to what I've got in store for you." She read him the Charlie scenario.

"So my cowlick is endearing?" he said with an angelic batting of his eyes.

"Shut up, Charlie."

"Actually, Emmaline, I think them becoming me is going a bit too far. Aren't they just supposed to adore us so the outcasts become the admired? I thought the point is our anxiety of non-acceptance disappears."

"Yeah, something like that. I just thought it was fun to take it all the way to its most horrifying conclusion. Can you imagine a million mini-me's?" She giggled. It felt great to release her nerves.

"Well, I hope Jensen and whoever else pounces on us lacks your lurid imagination."

"We'll know in fifteen minutes. I better check email before we go."

They turned back to their desks.

=

When Charlie and Emmaline arrived on the set they appeared calm and seasoned. Below the surface their combined heart rates could've pumped enough water to power the western seaboard.

"Ah, here they are," Jensen greeted. "Please sit down at the front here," he began directing them. Energy oozed from his compact frame.

There was an audience of six. Or at least it felt like an audience. It was actually a committee, put together to refine the idea and make sure it fit with the properties of the new product. Arnie waved at them and gave a double-thumbs-up, wink and nod.

"So," continued Jensen, "we'll do a little screen test today to see how you photograph, but mostly we'll work through the final concept and storyline for the ads. The scenario so far is you're attractive misfits going out into the world, and when you get there, far from being outcasts, the world will be drawn to you. You will end up showing a strong comfort level in your surroundings. We will coach you to look anxious at the beginning and to psychologically bloom as the world responds positively to you."

"Is that what you were thinking, Benson?" Jensen addressed the small man in a grey suit. "Benson is with us from Product Development," he put in as an aside before the man could answer.

"Well, yes. I got excited about this idea at the initial meeting, although I'm concerned this may not show the idea of making the client feel at one with their surroundings well enough. The pharmaceutical brings one into psychological harmony with others by making them feel they are similar. That's why Development named it *Assimilaire*. When we discussed it this morning in our department, we were concerned the proposal didn't show enough conformity. We think sameness should be shown visually."

Emmaline raised her hand. "But the whole thing that carries the campaign is that you can be yourself and feel accepted, due to the effect of this wonder drug."

"Well, Development is willing to see if you can act Accepted well enough to illustrate the concept conclusively. I personally can't imagine how it will be communicated without visual conformity." Benson replied.

"Okay, Emmaline," Jensen directed. "Up on stage. Marlene and Ina, will you please join her and play the other parts. Let's give it a try."

She wobbled with nerves as she mounted the two steps, trying her best to imagine it was just another marketing presentation.

"So here's the scenario: You walk into a crowded gallery carrying your sketches. The patrons are high-brow and the gallery is snooty. You appear to be a street artist with a hesitant but fairly confident air. You walk directly to the owner and present your work. She oo's and ah's and shows a sketch to her partner who holds it up to the patrons who swarm around you with handshakes and looks of awe. You smile in ease, and the camera comes in tight on your relaxed, confident smile. Then we cut to product branding and info."

"But..." Benson began.

"Just wait a minute, Benson, let's see what it looks like," Jensen insisted.

"Can I have a folder to hold?" Emmaline asked in a voice barely audible.

Charlie, bounded up with her briefing notebook and quivered as he gave it to her. His quaking hand completely unnerved her.

She took a deep breath, held her head up and began walking forward toward the other ladies. At least she didn't have to speak. Ina contracted her dark features into a snobbish sneer and pretended to look at artwork on invisible walls. Marlene, her red hair pulled into a tight bun, stood tall with a raised eyebrow. Emmaline approached eyebrow-woman and handed her the notebook, remembering not to set her back to the audience. She forgot to do anything with herself while the woman reviewed her portfolio. Eyebrow-woman smiled and opened her vividly-painted lips in mock delight. She sailed across the stage with one torn out sheet of paper held up before her, and the other woman made an 'oo' shape with her lips and nodded. They came smiling over to Emmaline and gave her bobble-headed approval.

"Okay, cut," Jensen called, waving his short arms like a penguin, "we get the idea. Whadda ya think Benson?"

"Well, I can see the approval, but the artist doesn't look comfortable. Her shoulders are around her ears and she's shaking with nerves."

"We can work on all of that. It's her first run-through, and she's not a trained actress."

"Yes, I can see that." He paused. "Even if the performance is flawless, I'm not sure I'd be convinced or connect it to the medication. For one thing, they are really approving her work, not her."

"Hmm. Point well taken." Jensen paused.

Benson spoke up. "I think we need a more radical show of conformity. Instead of presenting work, maybe she could walk into a park filled with families and tourists, and when she sets up an easel and begins to paint, they all put down what they're doing and pull out easels and begin to paint too. When they smile a chain of smiles in her direction, she smiles back and in a chain, they each become dressed like her with features like her. She glows with joy and paints with great strokes of confidence."

"Wow, that's great!" Jensen enthused, "Why have you been hiding in Development, Benson? You should adopt him on your team, Arnie."

Arnie grinned and gave a thumbs up.

"Much more dramatic and to the point, don't you think, Emmaline?" Jensen challenged.

"I uh...don't know." Her voice was small.

"It's fabulous!" he confirmed.

"Well," said Benson, "It's just in Development we kept discussing the theme of sameness. When you are the same, you are identified with a group, and they accept you. In animal studies, there was an elevated anxiety level if an animal was made to wear a strange marking or piece of clothing when it entered a group of its own kind. When the marking was removed and it entered again, the anxiety level was much lower and the acceptance level was higher. The medication was created to produce the chemicals we found in humans when they felt identity with or acceptance in their group - sameness. It only makes sense to show them visually the same to illustrate the identity and social ease. We adjusted our concept - to accommodate Marketing - to have others become like our subject instead of our subject become like others, but the visual likeness seems imperative."

"But the drug won't really make them the same," Emmaline countered, suddenly confident in her usual role. "So wouldn't it be false advertising to make the people become too much like them?"

"Emmaline, you're in Marketing Concepts. Your whole career is the creation of smoke and mirrors to illustrate an abstract point. We can't possibly show what the drug really does. And we can have Legal create any disclaimers that may be necessary. That's just part of the pharmaceutical game. No worries there." Jensen assured her.

"Come on down, ladies," he continued. "Let's talk over a scenario for the handsome young climber here."

Emmaline was more wobbly leaving the stage than she had been on the way up. Everyone morphing into her - it was nightmarish! She'd created that scenario for Charlie as a joke to tease him. They couldn't be serious!

"Hey," Ina piped up behind her on the steps, "this is pretty good." She flipped her long black braid and handed the piece of paper Marlene had torn from Emmaline's notebook to Jensen.

Emmaline's pained eyes flew to Charlie's face. She shook her head and raised her brows in hopeless apology.

"Yeah, not bad, Emmaline. Apparently we should've asked for your latest suggestions before creating the scenario this morning. This is right in line with Benson's great idea. Guess he's not taking your job after all." Jensen's glittering eyes were anything but reassuring to her.

She felt faint. She brought that along to give to Charlie, to rub in the joke after they were done with the morning's discomfort. Now she'd be credited with this disaster. Why not just promote cloning to make the world a safer more comfortable place for all. Even if the clones were as lovable as Charlie, it would be too much of a good thing! She sat down and tried to get her heart to stop racing as Jensen read her monstrous creation to the rest of the group.

= NINE =

The rest of the session was standard. They took headshots, worked on blocking, projection and expression, and talked about wardrobe. Marlene from Ad Production gave each of them some coaching and exercises to practice. Odd that they had to learn to be themselves.

Emmaline was relieved to hear it would take a week to put up the final set, even in rush mode. She and Charlie would be sent a script and then be called back in to practice blocking on the set. They'd need to smooth up the final performance before shooting. But there would be one whole week of normalcy - she hoped.

It was almost lunch time. She noticed the downpour out the front façade as she passed and realized she would have to duck back into her office to grab her coat and boots. A delay before going out for something to eat and a much needed escape. She had tried to avoid Charlie by milling around after they were dismissed. She knew he'd be out of there like a shotgunned bear to retreat to his cave and lick his wounds in their private sanctuary. Emmaline just didn't want to hear it. He was going to kill her!

She slunk in, all but slithering to avoid the sound of footfalls. Maybe he would be so absorbed he wouldn't notice her.

"Nice job, Emmaline," he threw out in a mocking tone.

"Oh, Charlie, I'm so sorry. I never dreamed it would take this tack. I thought it would be cool and easy and..." she felt herself redden with remorse and embarrassment. She had let him down and thrown herself in the sinking ship with him.

"Take it easy there, Em," the affectionate term slipped out. He stumbled, "um, it really isn't that bad. It's just a commercial." He saw her face flushed like a puffed-up tomato, and she looked ready to cry. "It'll be over before we know it."

"You're not going to yell at me?" she ventured, afraid to believe it.

"Why would I yell at you? Have I ever yelled before?"

"Well, I didn't mean it literally, but I thought you'd be really pissed."

"Actually, I think it's kind of funny. Can you imagine a whole world full of you and me?" His face broke into the most wonderful smile, and he laughed louder than usual.

She pressed her lips in a shy smile and looked down and then up at him. "Yeah, I guess it is kind of funny to think about. I'm so relieved you're not upset at me for getting us into this."

"Well, it wasn't your idea to put us on stage - at least not directly. And I know you didn't mean that mess of a scenario to fall into their hands…"

"I can't believe they took that seriously!" she interrupted, back to her more jovial self.

"Well, considering they had just made up the same thing for you, of course they thought it was brilliant."

They laughed together, their tension dropping away.

"What do you say I join you out for lunch today?" Charlie offered.

She had been about to call him on the 'Em' thing, but dropped it along with her jaw. In a brief second she recovered. "Sure," she replied like it happened every day. "You know it's raining buckets out there."

"Yeah, okay, it is Seattle in November and all."

They bundled up and headed out into the slate grey deluge - Emmaline bouncing along like it was the first sunny day of Spring.

"Where are we going?" he remembered to ask when they were down the block.

"Cajun Corner?" she tried.

"Oo, yeah - red beans and rice. But am I going to have to watch you eat one of those disgusting burgers?" he teased.

"Yup, medium rare and smothered in Tiger sauce. I'll bite down really hard so you'll have to watch the blood ooze out." Her eyes shone like drops of starlight.

"Meat is murder!" he said at a Charlie-shout, barely audible over the passing cars.

"Oh, Charlie, don't be a drama queen. I've seen you eat it in a pinch." All in good fun. She knew Charlie was vegetarian for world resource management and personal health rather than animal rights activism. He'd eat anything before he'd let it go to waste.

He dropped the point as they walked under the awning by the door, and he opened it for her with a flourish. "After you, my dear Carnivore." He smirked.

=

They settled back into their Batcave. Once more the secret haven of comfort, removed from the craziness of their corporate surroundings. Charlie had plenty to do in refining the package design now that the packaging department had decided on material and the teams had hammered out the text. He had already decided to suggest an irregular shape for the boxes that would fit together when stacked.

Emmaline sifted through emails, in a flurry of give and take on finalizing the commercial script and creating the copy for the print campaign. Charlie's decision to treat it as a romp had lifted the shadow from her in dealing with the whole thing. Looking back over the last twenty-four hours, she wasn't sure what had made her take it so seriously in the first place. It's not like people were really going to become her, and the stage acting might be fun. It was certainly a change from brain-busting ad copy creation. She smiled as she watched the clock tick down the back side of the day.

"Oh my, God! It's Thursday," she blurted out.

"Oh my, God," Charlie mimicked. "You're right." He kept designing.

"I'm supposed to go see Boogie Brown with Sarah tonight. I can't believe I forgot. I better get psyched up. I'm gonna meet her down there."

Charlie gave up for the day, pulling out and shutting down. "What psyched up? You've seen him a million times, and it's reggae dancing. You could probably do it in your sleep."

"Yeah, actually it will feel great. I just was thinking I was staying home, that's all." Her eye sparked under a lifted brow. "Wanna come?"

"Yeah, right." He gave her a twisted smile as he plugged his iPod into his head-sockets and got up for his coat. He turned and spun his hand open in a rounded five motion as he retreated out the door.

"Guess that's the end of that." She chuckled to herself. She would've fallen on the floor if he'd actually wanted to come.

Emmaline, bundled up in boots and coat, entered the Real World humming a tune with a reggae sound. The gloom of the street rolled off her like the forgotten stress of the day.

= TEN =

A week had passed and the campaign for *Assimilaire* was taking shape. Charlie's elegant logo was now integrated onto an irregular, slanted rectangle box. He had seemed peeved when they made a regular block when stacked opposite each other, but his mood had picked up when he got to create the design to be printed in reverse on half of the boxes. Two designs were necessary in production to have the correct face on the shelf from the front when the boxes were stacked in alternating directions on top of each other. It would make the stockers crazy to receive two cartons with each new order and have to stack them every other one. Different to be the same.

Emmaline was finessing the scenarios, working on the final wardrobe. She tried not to think about their session later that morning. They were starting filming! How silly to think about what she wore to an art opening or to paint in the park in such excruciating detail. It was counter-intuitive to scrutinize the expression of the artistic soul in such a fashion. It made it seem like it was exactly that - fashion. She wore whatever felt right. She didn't have a style. And yet, when putting together wardrobe, it turned out she did. There were recognizable items that cried, Artist. She had to hit up friends for their 'mirrors' to see herself, but they told her what she wore without hesitation. They all came up with the same basic items. Pea coat, boots, often a wool beret or other hat that added a splash of color, some kind of interesting scarf or a hand painted t-shirt. Gauzy blouses with embroidered patterns. Flannel pants.

Lots of stripes and plaids and patterns of harmonious hue mixed with unity in their chaos. She sighed.

Arnie burst through the door - a terrible intrusion at over an hour before they were to be frog-marched to the set. "Good morning, my special, amazing, artistic geniuses!" he enthused. "I have an announcement so awesome it just couldn't wait for the shoot today."

Emmaline and Charlie looked like they would prefer to be shot literally than to hear his awesome announcement.

"Marcus just called Joe to say that our campaign has been chosen for an award - specifically the two commercial scenarios starring Charlie," he paused to fling his hand out dramatically, "and Emmaleen," other hand flung outward, "who are to travel for a presentation live at...You'll never believe it..." he bubbled to their green faces, "the Chicago WWPA Con! In just a couple weeks!!"

"That's right!" Arnie took their shocked, gaping mouths to be open in astonished delight. "You've won Worldwide Pharmaceutical Association recognition in the Breakthrough Ad Concepts category! We rock!!" he all but screamed.

They all but screamed too - without making a sound. He didn't seem to notice his was a rockin' party of one.

"See you at the shooting!" he oozed as he patted Charlie on the back and – thankfully - left them on their own.

The silence ached with terror for what seemed like hours before Emmaline wailed, "Oh, Charlie!"

"Yup, this isn't funny anymore," he confirmed. "Let's just work quietly and pretend this never happened until time to go get shot, and if it turns out Arnie's announcement is true, we'll ask them to use real bullets."

She couldn't even manage an obliging snicker, as she turned to her monitor and gazed at Charlie's wardrobe list with unseeing eyes.

=

Jensen jumped back from the door as Charlie and Emmaline rushed through it two minutes late. "Come on you two. None of these actors' bad habits like tardiness. I expect more of you. And for

Pete's sake relax a little. This is not going to hurt. You don't even have lines. Just smile. Your screen tests ranked high on charisma. You're gonna do great."

Emmaline went to the point, "Have you heard anything about a live performance, Jensen?"

"Oh...that. Now who would've spoiled your nerves before a shoot by spilling a thing like tha..." he followed their miserable eyes to where they fastened on Arnie, who waved at them in excitement. "Great." Jensen dropped. "Well, you'll just have to make the best of it. I know this is going to be harder to pull off now that you think you're on a world stage. Just pretend that won't be happening. Chances are today's scene won't be used for that kind of thing anyway, so just forget about tomorrow and act your asses off. Get up front and let's get started." He turned and announced. "Okay people - places!"

The morning wore away. They had walked through their scenes a dozen times, getting their blocking to flow, perfecting their body language and those charming smiles. The bit actors had it down. Charlie and Emmaline were struggling. They just couldn't find the fun in it anymore. And at this point Emmaline was starving. They weren't going to lunch until two.

"Cut, cut," Jensen hollered after an especially awkward run-through. "Take a break." He waved the two stars over to him.

"Okay, kids, I know you can do this. Emmaline, I've seen you glow like a roman candle when you're fired up about a presentation, and Charlie, you're the poster-child for Cool and Calm. You've got to forget everything except this moment. You get to be king and queen of make-believe. You're the people that everyone admires—that everyone wants to be. Take it into your imagination. Have fun with it. Think, *Assimilaire*. Ease. Comfort. The whole world is yours. It conforms to you. Everything you love, it loves. Every song played is your favorite. Only your desires matter now."

As silly as it sounded, Jensen's suggestion worked. He led their artistic inspiration and got them to flow with it. The scenarios fell into place, smooth as a seal in a vat of Crisco.

"It's a wrap!" The glorious words fell from Jensen's tongue at two-thirty-five. "Take lunch people! You get an extra half hour for taking it late and a job well done."

Charlie and Emmaline headed back toward the changing area to put on their corporate clown-suits. "Seems kinda funny we're changing out of our normal clothes and into something else when we're finished acting," he noted to Emmaline.

"Hey, wait you two," Jensen called as he approached. "Don't bother to change unless you want to. You're off for the rest of the afternoon."

Their smiles amped up a notch.

"There's just one more thing."

Charlie's eye brow rose skeptically.

"Arnie's untimely announcement is dead on." He didn't wait for their reaction. "After today's performance I know you will have nothing to worry about. We'll be working together on it, and I can get you confident and relaxed. It'll be a lark. It's all in how you approach it. Especially since you don't have the pressure of really wanting to be stars, I think you'll find the big stage an intoxicating experience. It's a hoot. So be back for rehearsal on Monday. We've taken the concept and developed some ideas for the show. You'll have input of course. We have two weeks to polish it up. Piece 'o cake. Have a good weekend!"

"What are we a bunch of birds?" Charlie snarked when they were out of earshot. "A hootin' lark. Great."

"Hey, don't be so negative. That's my job," she teased.

He eased up a little. "You mean you're on board?"

"Do we have a choice?"

"Good point. I guess we may as well make the best of it."

"Maybe it actually will be fun."

"Yeah." He was completely unreadable.

"Sucks about Thanksgiving though," she pointed out.

"Thanksgiving?"

"Yeah, the WWPA Con is Thanksgiving weekend, and I'm sure they'll fly us out Thursday to be there for the big Friday kick-off."

"Saves me having to watch everyone at my Sister's savagely mutilating and swallowing an innocent turkey."

"Give it up, Charlie."

He grinned as they entered their work abode.

"What're you gonna eat? I'm ravenous!" she said.

"Do ravens hoot? Oh, sorry. Um. I've got some hummus and bagels here."

"Thrilling."

"Okay, Ace, where are you takin' me this time? Let's whoop it up. They let us out early."

She thought on her feet. "Melting Pot?"

"Oooo. How trendy." He looked non-plussed.

"Have you ever been? I know it sounds corny, but it's really good. And we can go all veggie…well some cheese will be involved. You haven't gone vegan on me now have you?"

"No. Dairy is a renewable resource."

"Jerk."

"Okay, okay. Take me to your fondue."

"And there'll be chocolate…"

She saw his eyes spark. He tried to be cool about it, but she knew Charlie was an insatiable chocolate fiend. Good man.

They donned their layers for the bus ride across town to Queen Anne. The crisp air met them as they stepped out of their corporate confinement. Small, billowy clouds punctuated the clear blue waterfront skyline. Glorious!

"Let's walk!" she commanded in a joyous tone that could not be denied. She jumped forward with the solidity of a fine horse tempered with her trademark element of grace.

They covered the distance — taking a shortcut through Seattle Center - chatting away about everything except *Assimilaire* and the upcoming campaign trail. Emmaline whirled around looking up under the Space Needle until Charlie had to catch her dizzy self. 'Tradition', she called it. And Charlie insisted they walk down into the fountain until they could feel its spray.

As they shared their early dinner - cooking food in a common pot - they knew whatever was ahead would be alright if they did it together. Maybe it would indeed be 'a hoot.'

= ELEVEN =

The next two weeks were full of rehearsals and endless emails riddled with tweaks and polishes on the presentation for WWPA Con. Emmaline got sucked into the vortex of creativity and theatre and seemed to lose all trepidation of the stage. Charlie, on the other hand, was left out of the process and had to adapt to the changes each time they went through the performance. He poked at designs for upcoming releases, but there was nothing to keep him occupied - or distracted. His nerves intensified rather than relieved with each run-through.

Emmaline's ease denied Charlie the release of commiseration and left him feeling isolated. The bond they had shared at dinner melted away. She was oblivious - laughing and one-upping with Ina. He had checked himself for jealousy and was sure it wasn't that. He just didn't like the idea of being in the spotlight. Even for a few minutes. Even in another city.

The commercials would debut on television at the same time they gave the big presentation at WWPA Con, so at least he wouldn't be famous before he left town. Charlie cringed in his chair at the thought of coming home and being recognized on the street. He tuned in to his computer and drifted off to his favorite music site. Drowning his fears with Skinny Puppy through the gurgling sounds of Emmaline's hearty laugh coming in from the water cooler.

"Guess what, Charlie?" Emmaline blurted - unceremoniously loud when she re-entered the office.

He began to pull himself out of his muse as she continued.

"Mlmma rhm blbba new idea for you to add to the script," he heard as he emerged. "You're gonna love it. You get to ad lib on how you feel when you crest a ridge."

"Um, can you just write some copy for me? I'm sure you'll capture the feeling."

"But don't you want to contribute to your unique identity? I thought that's what you find cool about the campaign."

"You know me well, Emmaline. You can do it. I can't find my identity in the cool campaign. I can't relate to anything about it anymore."

Charlie's morose figure cut through the shimmery film of her creative bubble. He was agitated! "I'm sorry, Charlie. You're really out of sorts, aren't you?"

"Well….yes," he allowed a pout to occupy his features, a rare occurrence.

"When did this happen? I thought we were having fun?"

"That ship sailed at least a week ago for me. The tighter the presentation, the tighter the knot between my shoulders. I don't know if I can pull this thing off. I feel ridiculous. It's just not me."

"But we've worked so hard to make it exactly you," she said in a sympathetic tone.

"Maybe that's exactly the problem. I'm not used to working to be like me. I'm just me. Being on stage as uber-Charlie is a horrible exercise in exaggerated self-examination. I don't like being bigger than life. I'm so aware. Everyone has scrutinized what makes Charlie, Charlie, and then instructed me on how to be Charlie in so many ways that I can't find myself at all. When I'm off stage my psyche heads for the archetypal hills. It's like living beside myself."

"Wow," Emmaline pulled up nearer to him in her chair. "It's not like that for me at all. I mean, I can't say it's not unsettling, but I like the self-discovery. I never realized I had a style. I never knew I was considered successful or admirable."

"That part's okay. It's the smaller stuff, like when they tell the other actors to look more geeky or lanky, not so classically suave, when they're supposed to mimic me. I didn't know I looked geeky. I mean, I know I *am* geeky, but I thought I looked athletic."

"You do look athletic, Charlie. Jen thinks you're hot."

"Great. See. That's what I mean. I don't want to know that. You never would've told me that when I was just Charlie. Now it's gonna be weird."

"Well, you seemed to need reassuring."

"I never needed reassuring when I was just being myself. I feel like I'm in a hall of mirrors and every one of them makes my ass look big - so to speak," he finally cracked a crooked snigger.

Emmaline laughed in relief. "You're gonna be fine, Charlie. Even though it seems like we're amplifying your quirks, it's really our perceived - as you say - uber-Charlie. It has little to do with the real you, which is far too complex, creative and changeable to ever portray in a forty second commercial or fifteen minute presentation. Relax and be yourself. I'll write the copy for uber-Charlie. You're right. You're not him, and there's no reason I can't write his script better than you can."

Charlie smiled and eased back into his surfing cockpit. He grabbed the console and after a smooth take off, flew away.

=

Charlie and Emmaline boarded the plane, the flight strangely empty. Maybe it wasn't such a bad thing to fly on Thanksgiving morning after all. It certainly worked for Charlie. She watched his long legs unfurl into the aisle, his face exuding pleasure in the luxury.

Chicago. It couldn't have been Lisbon or Paris or, anywhere but Chicago? Emmaline sat back in her seat and yanked off her too-heavy coat that she'd need when they arrived. She pulled out her cross-stitch. Good thing there was no point on the needle, they probably would've confiscated such dangerous contraband. She smirked at the thought of taking over a plane by needlepoint. Instead of sewing, she stared out at the tarmac from her window seat, anxious about take-off. She used to love flying. Still did, but her fears had grown along with her understanding of the foibles of humanity. So many things to go wrong. She comforted herself by accepting it was beyond her control. 'Eat, drink and be merry for tomorrow you may die.' She always liked that one. She could feel it in her bones. Can't change it, so love it with all you've got. Still her needle stayed idle till they were in the air.

She looked over to see Charlie's ears full of iPod as usual, but he looked asleep. At least he wouldn't see her cross-stitching like a mid-western school marm. She giggled to herself. So much for the cool and successful uber-Emmaline.

The chime brought the pilot's voice to rouse Charlie with the 'ten minutes until landing' notice. He pulled out extra slow, and Emmaline ditched her stitching before he was coherent. They had a smooth landing and deplaned in record time with the small load.

"Now where?" Emmaline demurred.

"Well, we can skip baggage claim," he held up his compact, canvas overnight bag. Their wardrobe for the show and cocktail hour formals were being shipped out along with the rest of the set, so they only had to bring basics. They were to fly back on Saturday morning. Emmaline lugged her bulging-to-bursting gym-style bag toward the taxi area as Charlie pointed out the icons to lead the way. Their bags were restricted to stowable size, but they didn't say anything about how heavy they could be. She was a be-prepared kind of gal, and although adventurous, she always nested wherever she landed - even for a day.

"The Milieu midtown," Charlie instructed the cabbie. They both looked out their windows at the passing streets without conversation - used to being together in their own inner spaces. At this point it was all just something to see. A waiting game for what lay ahead.

Charlie paid the cab with his company card. She eased back from her urge to control. She had a thing about tips. She had worked in the service industry as a picture framer for awhile, and she knew the energy it took to give people a smile all day long.

A smile volunteered itself as she appreciated Charlie's generosity. Although, it wasn't his money anyway, she realized.

"Would you have given him that big of a tip if you were paying?" she asked as they walked to the door.

Charlie looked embarrassed as the bell hop glanced at her while supplying them a cart. "Oh no, that's okay," he waived it away. "We've only got one thing each."

Emmaline hiked up her lump of lead and soldiered on.

"Yes, I would've given him the same tip, Emmaline. But do you mind keeping it down a little. I didn't want to give one to the bell hop too, and you made it a little awkward."

"Hmph," she didn't get it.

"I'll check us in," she offered as they approached the counter.

=

Charlie stepped back and went to admire the floral shop that presented as an exotic terrarium onto the promenade in the mezzanine of the hotel. Their arrangements had the balance of asymmetry that Charlie grooved on. And he loved flowers. Arranging them was a passion he mostly kept hidden, much like Emmaline and her stitchery.

A wild waggling motion caught the corner of his eye, and he saw Emmaline swinging her whole arm in a come-over-yonder. He had never noticed how extreme she was in public. But then, they hadn't spent much time together out of the office. She still had grace of movement, but she was a bit brash in relating to strangers. Maybe she got wild when she was nervous or something. It would be an interesting couple days.

She held up his card-key like a doggie treat as he approached. As they headed for the elevator he started thinking maybe his perspective was skewed by his nerves instead of it being her behavior. It was innocent enough to hold the card in the air for him to reach it. "I'm feeling a bit punchy," he admitted. "I think I might take a shower or something and meet you later."

"We could go for a sauna or sit in the hot tub?" she suggested on their ride to the fourth floor.

"No, maybe later. I just wanna veg for a bit on my own. Sorry to be a poop."

"No worries. I'm a big girl. I can find my own way to the pool."

He walked down the hall to his room, and she walked the other way to hers. "Okay, ring my room when you're feeling sociable, 4023." she called back to him and saw him nod in agreement.

=

A swim did sound delicious. The only thing about the hotel she had drooled over online was their three-lane lap pool. She hoped everyone would be gorging themselves with Turkey Day stuffing and she'd score a spot without delay. She dropped her bag on the bed and changed. Then sighed as she viewed her suited-up self in the mirror. Not the figure she'd once had. But she wouldn't let imperfection keep her from something she loved. It wasn't a fashion show. She pulled on her sweats, that would double as her jammies later, and headed out.

The water was perfect, and she felt the stress of travel flow off her body as she slipped through, secure in its encompassing arms. In Miami, she had grown up in the water. She couldn't remember a time when she couldn't swim. Well, unless you count the few years she spent in retreat from the freezing lakes of the Northwest or their stuffy, chemical-stinky indoor pools. Swimming outdoors in naturally warm waters was hard to let go of. But eventually the draw of floating through an atmosphere pulled her back into the deep end, and she had become obsessed. She swam every morning at five a.m. sharp for several years. The meditative euphoria embraced her again now, and she lost all sense of time and place. Just moving and breathing in a world of her imaginings. Paradise.

She got out, refreshed, and remembered the other thing she loved about working out in the pool. Every muscle felt relaxed yet charged. She was tired like the end of a satisfying day, and energized like waking from a long and fabulous dream.

Back at her room, she showered and then checked messages. Charlie had called about ten minutes before. Emmaline toweled off her hair and tamed her curls with spicy Moroccan oil. She breathed in the sandalwood-like aroma and gave a luxurious stretch before calling him back.

"Hey Charlie," she greeted. "Ready to turn Chicago on its ear?"

"Yeah, right," she heard him smile. "I would like to leave my room now, though."

"Okay. Did you happen to check in with Joe? I just remembered we were supposed to call when we were settled in."

"Yup, got it. And I already had our shipped clothes sent up to my room. We're to meet Joe tonight at seven for dinner. We don't have to get in our costumes - our cocktail formals, I mean - but he said to look nice. We'll be hobnobbing with some Pharmy reps."

"Oh, great. Good thing I brought my silk skirt. It rolls up into a little scroll and rolls out to dinner wear."

"Got a matching monkey-suit for me in your bag o' tricks?"

"You're on your own, pahtna," she grinned. "You did bring something to dress in didn't you, Charlie?"

"Yes, mother," he intoned dryly.

"Sorry," she sounded sincere. "So gimme about twenty minutes. I was gonna say ten, but I better do a bit of extra work now if I'm to look nice later."

"Please, don't rush your beauty secrets on my behalf," he teased. "I'll head down to the mezzanine and order up a smoothie. Want one?"

"Oooo. Sounds perfect after my swim. I was thinking coffee, but you're brilliant. Vitamins ace caffeine any day of the week - if I would just remember that."

"Berry, right?"

"Hey, you're good. Have you been spying on me?"

"Um, I'm the guy who sat at the desk across from you for - how many years?"

"Four, but who's counting." Emmaline was smiling to a shine.

"See you in a few, Batgirl." She could tell he was smiling too. Her mind's eye caught the glint in his warm baby-browns.

= TWELVE =

Charlie and Emmaline laughed their way through the streets of Chicago. They wrapped up in their coats and scarves like mummies and played tomb raider on the sidewalk. They got a snack at a 'famous' bagel shop and looked in store windows. Neither one was taken with the façade of the street. It was just like any other city around its tourist core. Chain stores, high end boutiques and gimmicky shops with lots of post cards. They made the best of it, but nothing seemed to jive with them. Undoubtedly their preferred type of haunts lay in another part of town.

They were almost back to the hotel to get ready for dinner, when things went awry.

"Quit staring, Emmaline," Charlie stage whispered with a sidelong glare at her.

"Oh, sorry," she glanced at him, and then her eyes strayed back to their target in fascination. She focused on the man with permanent crutches. "I'm not judging him or anything; it's just intriguing to see how he gets along in such a different way. I'm admiring him actually. That takes a lot of strength - and courage. It's amazing…"

"Knock it off."

His tone stopped her in her tracks. "Sorry, Charlie." she looked in his eyes. "I really don't think he noticed me. I didn't mean to offend anybody." Her face squeezed in confusion. She'd never heard Charlie chide her so harshly.

"Oh, he noticed. His whole life is spent under scrutiny."

"What's the matter with you, Charlie? I wasn't scrutinizing, well, other than how well he had worked out his movement. Like I said, I find it amazing."

"It's not amazing, Emmaline. It's brutally difficult, and the hardest part is having everyone considering you - whether they decide you're freakish or brave. He's just trying to get some coffee or the paper. Leave him alone."

"Gee, Charlie. What brought that on?"

"I have experience."

She waited. Finally giving him the space he needed to express himself.

"I was born with slight palsy. I had to wear leg braces until I started school. I was also born loving to move, and I was determined to run and play and climb with the other kids. Most of them shunned me for walking funny. Being different at that age is the kiss of death. They called me Dork Boy and mimicked my jerky dragging that you deem an amazing way to get along. And, like you, my couple of accepting friends stared at me too. Morbid fascination, Emmaline. It's morbid. And if you want to justify it with saying you find it heroic, hold up a mirror to your face while you're frozen in admiration some time, and you'll see the tell-tale pity in your eyes. You're impressed but also upset that he has the balls to throw himself through life like that."

"I had no idea, Charlie, really." Emmaline let the bite of his drastic words drop away, understanding it was a bark of alarm guarding an old and deep pain. She remembered his insecurity about being called geeky and lanky. A couple words that went with dorky and awkward, perhaps. "And I truly do admire anyone that passes along streets that are paved with people who are very other than they are. I get your point about the staring though, no matter what I think my justification is. I couldn't stand it if someone stood gawking at me painting - even if it was in devoted admiration. I'd just be painting."

"And painting is something you're comfortable with. What if someone was watching you deal with one of your challenges in life."

"Ew, yeah, like when I'm on my tippie-toes flicking the corner of a cereal box on the top shelf at the grocery store hoping against hope it will move forward instead back. I feel completely vulnerable, and the thing I hate most in the world is when some well-meaning tall person comes around the corner as the box finally falls into my hands and says, 'Oh good job, I was about to come and help you.' I feel strange and ridiculous. I wish they would leave me alone. It's just part of being short. Nobody wants to be singled out like that. He was just walking somewhere like you and me."

Charlie nodded. She could see him go inward.

"And now you are the model for Climbing. I do admire you, Charlie. But you're not a freak, just a wonder. I'll try not to stare." The warmth in her voice was seductive.

He came back out to the surface and accepted her compliment with a soft smile. "But I don't want to be singled out for overcoming my adversity either. I'm just me."

=

They met in the hallway and took the elevator down to meet Joe and his entourage.

"You look great, Emmaline," he gave her. His eyes darted down and to the side.

She glowed in her turquoise silk skirt and jewel blue blouse and wore her four inch heels well, as much as she always whined about girl shoes. "Thanks, Charlie," she replied, oblivious to his shyness. "You clean up rather well yourself. Sorry about the mom thing earlier." Her brows went up and she rolled her eyes about with a smirk. She settled them back on him and was taken with the figure he struck. He had a fine physique when draped in well-tailored clothing. And navy blue was a great color on him. As much as she liked his green ribbed sweater, she was rethinking her preference for his style. Hard to imagine he ever felt gawky.

As they entered the lobby, they spotted Joe near the front desk. "Ah, here are our stars now," he welcomed. He introduced Marilyn Jennings, and Sharon Green, both marketing professionals from companies that were subsidiaries of their own.

The group crossed the mezzanine to the Palm Court, and as they were seated in a corner of the upscale eatery Emmaline felt intimidated and went inward, studying the women. Marilyn wore a dress of striking viridian green with a daring neckline. Her blonde straight hair brushed her bare shoulder with uncannily soft, sharp fringe. And she accented her lips with an unexpected dusky shade of burgundy. Sharon was a stunning woman with chocolate toned skin that held a hint of red lusciously blended in. Emmaline had to remind herself what Charlie had taught her about staring, even in admiration. It was all she could do to keep her eyes off Sharon's unusually rich complexion set off by her fine cream linen sheath dress. Her figure was fuller than Marilyn's but more appealing in many ways. And her shoes! They had the most divine texture. Corinthian leather? Emmaline wished she knew more about fashion so she would know what to ask for to find such gorgeous footwear. She was gushing like a - girl. Who knew? Emmaline felt underdressed, despite Charlie's compliment, but she soon forgot about herself as she was pulled into the conversation.

"How long have you been in Marketing, Emmaline?" Sharon was from London and carried a quick intensity behind her refined grace.

"Almost five years. Not much time really, but I've been a pitch gal all my life." Emmaline began to warm up. "I used to make up commercials for every item in the house as a child and was always critiquing the ads on TV. It was my mom who pushed me into the business. She had a journal filled with my ad one-ups, and when my picture framing career was at a crossroads she dug it out and got me excited about presenting my ideas."

Everyone laughed except Sharon. Her keen eyes recorded everything. It was apparent she would glean all she could from them. Emmaline made a mental note to keep her filter even if they had a couple drinks.

"I was glad when Samron Key opened in Atlanta. I was about five years into my career then," Marilyn spoke in a lovely drawl. "The next ten years were facinatin'. One success built on anotha' in the department, and I've been Marketin' Head for the last three years now. Our team has been together a long time, and we could use some fresh ideas."

Emmaline almost missed Sharon's next comment she was so surprised at Marilyn's implied age. She didn't look it. "Yes, we were highly impressed at Veroni Beckham when we heard of your success in creating an award-winning campaign. I hope you'll give us some preview information since we weren't privileged to be in on the selection committee for the awards this year." Sharon engaged Emmaline who broke the gaze and glanced to Joe.

"We need to keep the campaign under wraps, but we can give you a glimpse of the process or of what makes it different," Joe jumped in providing their parameters.

Charlie was silent, so Emmaline pulled herself away from savoring the prawns and tried to cut to the chase. "The concept was tied to the unique characteristic of the pharmaceutical itself. The basis of it is social comfort through feeling the same as those around you. When we approached the concept, we tried to avoid the obvious. Instead of having our socially stressed protagonist become like the others surrounding them, we chose to have society become like them."

"Yes," Marilyn responded, "we strive to avoid the obvious as well. But of course there's a fine line between creativity and becomin' too esoteric for your target market to relate to."

"Well, since our target market is those who don't fit in easily, an unusual approach should appeal to them very directly. At least that's our hope," Emmaline responded humbly.

"And what about design?" Sharon asked. "How do you create a design to correspond to the concept of the odd one being followed by the norm?"

Charlie shifted and pushed an asparagus spear across his plate.

"Charlie is our design man," Joe opened for him. "He can tell you how he worked through the dilemma."

"Well, uh, actually, I guess the design preceded the campaign idea. As Emmaline and I were in brainstorming, I came across something in some outside research I was doing. I'm interested in the Incan culture, and their stonework is remarkable. Each stone's unique shape is adapted into the building of the whole. They carved the stones slightly to fit together but avoided the static uniformity of modern bricks. The whole is stronger for the way they interwove the individuals into one unit."

"I love it when somethin' you're workin' on fits right into your assignment," Marilyn said. Her accent surrounded them in soft beauty.

"So would you consider it to be a fluke, then, this unique campaign idea?" Sharon asked. She didn't give an indication of whether she thought it was a good thing or a bad thing.

"No," Emmaline chimed in, "not a fluke. It was just an assignment given to the right designer at the right time. Having wide interests and being a research-oriented talent like Charlie contributed to its success. He made my job easy. Once he described how he interpreted the Incan stonework and showed me the elegant design he pulled from it, it was easy to extrapolate the rest. To keep the unique unique and change the norm to fit it. I love that it validates the strength of our clientele and offers them confidence that they can fit in as themselves. Be comfortable in their own skins. I think it would've been easy to portray the product as a way for them to avoid being themselves. But *Assimilaire* is supposed to make you feel comfortable with others. We think the heart of that concept is being accepted and loved for who you are."

"Hm, yes, I see how this is breakthrough - and excellent. You pulled this from an unusually deep but relatable place," Sharon ceded.

"Does it fit with the capability of the drug?" Marilyn cooed.

"You'll learn about that at the presentation tomorrow," Joe protected. "We don't want to steal Product Development's thunder."

They made it through dessert with amiable conversation. As Emmaline melted away the last dab of her chocolate mousse she flashed on how strange their dinner was in lieu of Thanksgiving dinner. No one ordered the turkey.

The group parted with the conventional 'nice to have met you' and 'thanks for dinner' and went their separate ways. Charlie excused himself to his room. Emmaline decided to go down to the hot tub. When she returned she noodled into bed, surprised at how relaxed she felt while anticipating the big day. She was off to dreamland with the script of being a star.

Charlie sat at his laptop far into the night surfing the comforting waves of cyberspace.

= THIRTEEN =

They entered the stadium-like conference room, awed by the stage full of set-up crew. Emmaline was glad Joe had picked them up in the lobby; her mind flipped like an over-easy egg that slipped to scrambled. "When are we up?" She sounded like a small child.

"They scheduled our presentation for ten o'clock," he said, "but we're to be ready to go at nine-thirty, just in case there are changes in the program. We'll take you backstage now so you know what to expect and where to meet before you go on."

Charlie yawned putting his elbow discreetly over his maw. Anyone would've thought he was cool as a cucumber, but he had just tired himself out to the point of having no hyper energy left to show.

Emmaline was at full spark. She arced higher at every point of their morning. "Will we get a run-through?"

"Not on stage," Joe informed, "but the IT guys will be set up for the PowerPoint and will meet you by nine. I would suggest finding somewhere to take a run-through."

Emmaline nodded, her eyes frozen open like she just saw Joe explode. He showed them where to come in later and led them to where they'd meet. Then he showed them the door of the stage entrance.

"Can we see through the door and try walking in?" Emmaline begged.

"I guess I can't see why not. There's still plenty of time before anything opens to the audience." Emmaline noted the time on his Rolex as he checked it at seven-thirty.

They opened the door onto an anthill of activity. The crew was scurrying about setting up mics and other equipment. Charlie lifted his eyes to the enormous monitor that backed the stage and would soon have his image filling it. He'd be acting in front of it in just a few hours. His knees quaked as if those early braces still shook his stability. He paced across the stage.

Emmaline saw it all as a canvas waiting for paint. Her fear dropped back behind her excitement. The day was finally here! The production they'd worked so hard on would come to the world stage. Charlie's and her campaign had gone international! They had television commercials play internationally before, but somehow it felt different to be there and present it herself. She looked off the stage and saw people were filtering into the auditorium. This was going to be one hell of a pitch! She was glad Jensen had roped them into this.

"Thanks, Joe. I feel oriented now." She glanced at Charlie and was surprised to see a wobbly ghost. She didn't embarrass him in front of Joe.

"Okay, so meet Jensen in the green room, no later than nine. He should be down there by eight-thirty if you need him. Like you, he was hoping to get the lay of the land before show time. Sorry I had to drag you out so early, but I need to be front and center with the other VP's when the program starts. I'll be busy with PR for us all day. I'll see your performance from the audience, but I won't be able to contribute. Break a leg, you two."

Charlie - the color of bleached flour - shook Joe's hand and turned to hone in on Emmaline's face.

She touched his shoulder, sensing he needed a stabilizing force. As soon as Joe was out of hearing range she whispered, "Are you gonna be alright?"

"I...I think so," he said, but looked unconvinced.

"We'll get you together before show time. Don't worry, it's almost over. Pretend it's a game show or something. Take the reality out of it. You are uber-Charlie now, remember?"

He smiled and the color began to return to his skin.

=

Charlie and Emmaline strolled along the sidewalk, pushing through the chilly wind to work off some nerves. Then they headed for the green room and a rendezvous with Jensen.

"Thank God!" Jensen cried when he saw them. "I thought you two would never arrive!"

"It's only one after. Joe told us to be here by nine," Emmaline checked.

"Nine! Doesn't give us much time for a run-through does it?"

The crowd erupted into such a roar of applause they could hear it through the walls.

Emmaline leaned up and whispered, "Go, uber-Charlie!" so that only he could hear.

He flushed and snickered.

"Okay, no time for clowning around, let's meet IT and run the script. We're going to be on before we know it," Jensen pushed, as he led them to another room.

"Uh, could you ease up a little, Jensen. We're nervous enough as it is. You said you'd make this easy and fun, remember?" Emmaline called after him.

"Oh, of course, and it is fun. I'm just excited that's all. Let's go lay it down! You guys rock!"

They hurried after his small frame, and Emmaline donned a wide smile. It was time for Arnie-esque enthusiasm. "Yeah, let's do it, Charlie!"

He followed, looking somewhat put together.

Emmaline waved at Jensen's assistant Ina, who gave her a thumbs up as she rushed off in the opposite direction.

They entered a generic-looking event room with busy-patterned carpeting and lots of wall sconces. Emmaline was surprised to see Marcus there. He had just flown in, replacing Benson, to do the product introduction. He was much more dynamic, so she saw it as promising but hoped it wouldn't throw Charlie off to have the last minute substitution. Marcus, from the Top office - this was a big deal! Her heart fluttered in fear which she told her brain was excitement, and she managed to catch her flighty breath.

Jensen used a diagram of the stage to show them their blocking. It was a good thing Emmaline had insisted they get a chance to walk on stage earlier. They ran through the script with a small PowerPoint accompaniment, complete with intro speech and all. Then it was potty breaks, any refreshments they could imbibe through their nerves, and back to the green room until show time.

=

Charlie and Emmaline perched on the luxurious red plush couches, unable to lean back into their comforting warmth. Charlie wondered in passing why the décor colors were red and gold for the green room. He knew green had a different meaning here, but the divorce of concept and design stuck in his craw. He removed his hat to keep from steaming in his own juices - wrapped and overdressed in his climbing gear.

"I wonder how the Top office's mass-sample suggestion will go over. I guess the *Assimilaire* and water have been given to the audience already. That's never been tried before," Emmaline mused.

"Yeah, it's daring and different." Charlie agreed. "I hope everyone takes them when Marcus tells them to so they have sympathy with me as a character."

"Oh, damn it Charlie. Really. Quit worrying. You've been fabulous at rehearsals, and there just isn't that much to go wrong. You don't even have any lines." His shoulders dropped down the tiniest of degrees from his ears.

Jensen had wandered off, but suddenly reappeared. "Ten minutes till we're on." He threw himself into the cushions of one of the far couches.

Charlie's shoulders returned to the region of his earlobes, and Emmaline shot off the couch and began pacing. As she got across the room near the main door, a woman entered and broke into a huge smile with her hand sticking forward.

"Well, you must be Emmaline," she said with a terrifying level of enthusiasm. "I've heard so much about you and the amazing campaign you have forged for your company's latest product, *Assimilaire*. I'm Zenia Curtz, a reporter for Pharmaceuticals Monthly." She nudged a black curl across her forehead with her knuckle. "I'd love to have a chat with you if you don't mind."

"Now?!" Emmaline spit out too loudly. Charlie's head swung toward her with a 'What the hell?'.

"Well, sure," replied the unquenchable Zenia. "It's as good a time as any."

"I'm about to go on." Emmaline explained.

"Oh, it won't take but five minutes. I know you're not going on before then."

"But…"

Charlie moved closer to her in sympathy with her anxiety. He hoped it would provide a distraction to calm his nerves.

"So, this product is unique in its potential to be sold over-the-counter at its release due to its remarkable lack of side effects and no detectable addictive properties throughout its trial period. How did you consider that wide open market in your campaign?" Zenia fired at her. Her too-pink lips formed a puckered rose.

Emmaline backed up from the recorder stuck in her face. "Um, since it is a mass-appeal product, we tried to relate it to everyone by making our models more accessible."

"Yes, but have you addressed the diversity of anyone and everyone being encouraged to try the new product for even the slightest feeling of discomfort?"

"Not r-really…I"

Jensen appeared at her elbow. "Uh, yes, I can field that one. Hello, Zenia. Jensen Roberts, Marketing Production Head for Schleagel-

Martin Pharmaceuticals." He jumped in and ran interference for his stars.

"Nice to meet you, Jensen. So you were saying?"

"We have an unprecedented surprise for our audience here at the conference that will unfold before your very eyes in about five minutes."

"Can you give me a sneak preview?" Zenia pried. She leaned in toward Jensen, daringly close.

"Well," his eyes raced from side to side before he mock-confided, "we are about to have our entire audience try a dose of *Assimilaire* before our presentation. It's been distributed to each person with their program. If that doesn't cry out safe and non-addictive, I don't know what does." He gave her a conspiratorial chuckle.

"Oh!" Zenia cried out in over-the-top delight. "This is better than I could have dreamed! And then what…"

"Oh, sorry Zenia…"

"But…"

"We really must go. We can talk later." He squeezed out from between her and the door where she'd boxed him in. "Let's go kids!" he shouted to Charlie, Emmaline and the crew. Marcus was already stepping through the stage door to take his place as the next speaker. They crowded out behind the curtain with him.

Emmaline gave Charlie an electric smile and squeezed his hand. Somehow the light in her eyes shimmered its way into his nervous system and lit his terror with excitement. He grinned back with relieved gratitude and pulled on his hat. "Break a leg, Emmaline," he whispered.

= FOURTEEN =

Charlie and Emmaline jittered with energy as they anticipated their cue. They focused on each word of Marcus' presentation speech:

And to go along with the novel concept of a pharmaceutical that provides social comfort, we have made it friendly in another way. It's the first time in history that a product of this type will be released directly to the over-the-counter market. Assimilaire passed all of its clinical trials and studies with a record so clean, that this marvel will have no listed side effects and can be advertised as completely non-addictive!

There was a pause for wild applause.

To celebrate this achievement, and because of the friendly nature of our product, we ask you to join with us and your fellow WWPA Con attendees to try a sample of our product en masse. You'll find your sample attached to your program. Please use our complimentary bottle of water by your seat to try the product at this time. Your only risk is feeling more at ease with your conference neighbor. Ready set Go!!!

Their theme song rang out through the auditorium and Marcus downed a pill as Emmaline and Charlie bounded on stage in their well-practiced, confident gait. They walked to the far edge of the stage waving and throwing out further samples, then took turns acting a stage version of their ads as first Emmaline's and then Charlie's commercials played on the screen backdrop. Jensen came out and read some details about the campaign, its conception and what made it so unique. Then he called Emmaline and Charlie to stand on each side of him as the President of the WWPA came out to give them their award. He shook their hands and Jensen turned to the mic to give their most humble thanks.

Then something completely unscripted happened. The president turned to Charlie and Emmaline and said, "I just have to do more than shake your hands. Perhaps it's the effect of this product I just took, but I feel that we're missing out if we let you leave the stage so soon."

They stood stunned as the audience again roared with applause.

"Please, Miss," he checked his program, "Emmaline Kinner, won't you tell us a bit about yourself and how you reached this illustrious point in your career?"

Emmaline's first impulse was to decline to comment, but when she glanced out she saw an audience at rapt attention and filled with encouraging expressions. She decided to go for it. "I... struggled as a visual artist and picture framer for several years and decided to try my hand at advertising. I had always been drawn to the world of Communications and hoped to add an artist's touch to the campaigns I was challenged with. I was given a chance to prove myself by Schleagel-Martin Pharmaceuticals, and ironically, by being my most humble self, I was elevated to this great position - given the chance to conceive this award-winning campaign in league with my partner Charlie Simon and the rest of our fantastic colleagues at Schleagel-Martin."

The crowd went mad with approval. She was pleased and dumbfounded.

"And Charlie, we know that you're a climber, but what else do you care about in life, and how did you end up on this stage today?" The President asked.

Emmaline thought it was a terribly intimate question for Charlie's sensibilities and wondered if he would have the courage to answer.

With a glance at Emmaline, Charlie began, "Well, I...um, I also enjoy music from the '80s new wave-punk era due to their emphasis on the importance of the individual in society. I think this campaign was conceived from...from my deep interest in how...

the uniqueness of individuals can be unified...to form a stronger societal structure than can ever be built through social conformity."

Emmaline was impressed and relieved at the confidence of his speech, but was cringing at the risk of his esoteric point, hoping he would draw applause.

He continued, "the fact that my company chose Emmaline and me to be the faces for the campaign played out the ideal within the concept in a way that we, as its creators, didn't dare dream possible. I am standing here today because I dared to be different...loudly."

The auditorium erupted into clapping, cheers, whistles and the mayhem of overwhelming support. The stars stood glowing with the intensity of the moment.

When the period of sustained clapping and standing ovation had passed absurdity, the President finally pointed Emmaline and Charlie to the door off stage. He then managed to quiet the crowd enough to announce, "That concludes our opening program. Please spend time at The Wickham's Linden Room enjoying our vendors, and be sure to attend our world-class seminars at The Milieu. Because of the enthusiasm shown toward Schleagel-Martin Pharmaceuticals' brilliant marketing designers, our dear Emmaline and Charlie, we will retain them in the green room for at least the next hour for a press conference and further questions on their lives and achievements."

His last sentence sunk in as Emmaline sunk into the now welcoming red cushions. "What?!" she shrieked, popping to the couch's edge.

"What?" Charlie asked in concern.

"He just said we'd be here for a press conference and questioning." She looked frantically at Jensen. "Is that true?"

"It is now," he chuckled with delight. "Great job! You're a hit."

"Great job, indeed," Marcus congratulated on his way by. "Take care with the press. I've got to run to the airport. See you back in Seattle!"

"Yeah, but..." Charlie began.

"Oh, don't worry Charlie, I'll go get you a plate of food before it's all gone. I noticed you hardly touched the buffet before the program." Jensen waltzed away.

"But…" Emmaline tried as Jensen shot her an opened mouth laugh and waved her to stay on the couch.

The two looked at each other in confusion. "What the hell happened?!" Emmaline emoted.

"It wasn't that great, was it?" Charlie asked her.

"Well, you were very eloquent in your answer, and I was proud of you for speaking up to all those people, but a standing ovation….It was kind of bizarre. I…"

Whatever she was going to say got drowned in a sea of people. They were swamped with a million questions from a jostling frantic mob. The first few through the door seemed unwilling to give up their positions next to the stars as more and more of them flooded into the green room.

The air was pierced by a fierce whistle that originated from Jensen. In the second of surprise it created, he shouted, "Ladies and Gents, we appreciate your enthusiasm, but we simply must get some order or we'll all be smothered. I and my assistant Ina are going to put you in a double file, one for Charlie and one for Emmaline. You'll be allowed two questions, and then you'll exit. If you don't co-operate, Jim and Max here will escort you out without a chance to meet them at all." He pointed to the Mack-truck-like hotel security guys.

Jensen and Ina started at the front creating a small space next to the newly risen stars. At last Emmaline could focus on the person in front of her. Charlie took a deep breath and looked like he wouldn't pass out after all.

"So how do you tame your curls, Emmaline?" the first woman asked. "I have a terrible time with mine." She stroked her slick, straight red hair.

Emmaline wasn't sure how to respond. She thought it a strange question but went for the straight answer. "Moroccan oil. It works wonders and smells terrific."

Charlie was experiencing the same oddities. The questions were personal and had nothing to do with pharmaceuticals or marketing. "What's your favorite punk band and why?" "Where do you buy your clothes?" And when he answered, their comments were even more surprising. "Yes, I can see where a small and practical apartment in the city would make me much happier too." "I have never read science fiction, but I'll stop on my way back to my room. What was that author's name again?"

It wasn't just the endless stream of conference attendees that had unusual questions for them either. The few reporters that were mixed in asked the damndest things. A gal from the Chicago Tribune asked, "What palette do you paint in?" And when Emmaline replied, she cried out, "I knew it. I could just see the cadmium and viridian green! And ochre - it makes such an expressive blend. The ochre so much subtler than yellow. So much deeper. I can feel it!"

Charlie and Emmaline worked their way through the lines. Each fan - for their zealous adoration allowed them to be named nothing else - would step away after their questions and the next was pushing forward to get their awaited turn. There wasn't a moment's peace to consult with each other or process the surreal situation.

At long last, the crowd waned. They answered the final two ridiculous questions and looked at each other, confirming at a glance that the other was just as bewildered. "What the freakin' hell?" Emmaline mumbled as the last man receded from them. She was too exhausted to exclaim.

"Yeah, that was more than a great campaign and an Oscar-winning performance would merit. 'Freakin' hell' says it all." Charlie agreed.

The plates of food that had been brought by Calvin and Ronny from their crew after the crowd was organized, sat untouched beside them. Charlie's was piled with ham and meatballs. He looked at it and scoffed. All the veggie stuff had been scarfed down first, the apologetic Ronny told him later.

There wasn't anything Emmaline preferred on her plate either, though they gave her one of everything left. Emmaline picked up a cold mini meat pie and chewed it, her face screwing up in disgust. "I'm starved," she admitted.

"Well I'm not eating this crap," Charlie spit out with uncharacteristic vehemence.

"Whoa, easy boy, I think we can sneak away for a snack of our choice now. We're done until cocktail hour reception and then we fly out, remember?" Emmaline offered.

"Oh, sorry Em, I'm bushed. Guess my blood sugar's at the breaking point."

She smiled as she caught him using the affectionate term. He didn't seem to notice.

"Alright, then pick up your hat and fleece and let's book," she said.

Just as they stood, Jensen came running in. "Oh, thank God you're still here. I've come to let you know you'll be staying for the rest of the conference...Well, if you possibly can, that is. And our Prez at Schleagel-Martin says to make you the offer that makes it possible. Jennings Foreman himself called me directly after Marcus reported in on his way to the airport." He looked desperate.

"Well, my first demand is a two hour lunch break," Charlie beat her to the punch.

"And mine is an explanation," added Emmaline. "What the hell is going on, Jensen?"

"It's a little late for lunch, I'm afraid, Charlie. It's four-thirty. But..."

"What?!" they shouted in unison. Even Charlie's voice rose to the occasion.

"I thought it just felt like that line went on forever," Emmaline moaned.

"No, it pretty much did," Jensen confirmed. "Of course you'll have time off. I insisted on the rest of the evening for you. You get to skip the cocktail reception. But they're hoping you'll agree to host a 'late-night' at the lounge."

"I don't drink," put in Charlie.

"Judging by this afternoon, I don't think you'll have time to anyway. They just want you to make an appearance. Apparently two questions each weren't enough for some folks."

"Okay, and my explanation?" Emmaline reminded.

"It is uncanny," Jensen agreed. "They're smitten with you. The conference committee wants you to stay and do two three-hour seminars tomorrow on 'Marketing a Successful Life.' The classes are already full with waiting lists, and they didn't even post them. That many people spontaneously asked to sign up for whatever you might be attending or teaching. Maybe it has something to do with the product as well as the design. They're really impressed."

"Can we walk, Jensen?" Emmaline suggested. "I think I'm going to faint if I don't get some decent food soon, and there's nothing left that either of us can eat here."

They glanced at the buffet as they passed and saw several trays nearly untouched. Emmaline became curious and pulled the guys aside. "Hey Charlie, if you could have chosen your plate yourself, would you have picked any of this?"

"Well, the only veggie left is pickled beets. I can't stand them."

"I don't like them either. And neither did any of those hundreds of people this afternoon."

His face lit, and he seemed to see her point. "Liver pâté? I remember one of your poetic soliloquies on the horrors of anything liver, rendered on a slow afternoon at the office. And God knows I wouldn't touch the stuff unless it was the last thing on earth."

"It is almost the last item left on the buffet." Emmaline turned to Jensen and Charlie, a tiny triangle of concern appearing between her brows. "Creepy," she stated.

Jensen laughed it off. "Come on you two. You must really be low on blood sugar. Let's get you over to Isadora's. I hear they have great vegetarian choices, and as far as I know, there's no liver pâté."

"No, Jensen, you don't understand," Emmaline explained as they pushed out into the hallway at last. "That's not the first strange thing we've seen this afternoon."

"Yes, I agree the huge press of people was a bit odd but…"

"Their questions were odder. I think about six of mine had anything to do with marketing or our product campaign. How about yours, Charlie?" she asked.

"Yeah, probably about the same - six, maybe eight."

Jensen's brow peaked in interest. "Then what the hell were you guys yammering about all these hours?"

"Hair product choices, favorite clothing shops, reggae music, artistic influences, how I dealt with the harshness of the world," listed Emmaline.

"Hiking boot preferences, band logos, the comparative joys of the city vs. mountain trails, favorite science fiction writers," Charlie added.

"Huh," Jensen grunted. It was his turn to look dumbfounded. After a moment he suggested, "You don't suppose it was the drug sample?"

"What else could it be?" Emmaline's eyes opened in fear. "Oh my God."

They walked along in silence.

"Do you think it will wear off?" Charlie asked at last.

"How do I know," Jensen replied, "but I'll get on the horn and find out if anything like this happened in the trials and studies."

"Yeah, maybe they didn't consider undue admiration a side-effect, but it's painful to me," Charlie said.

"And tell them it's a little beyond admiration perhaps," Emmaline added. "A lot of those people seemed to know too much about me. More than they could have gleaned from our short romp on stage. They understood the reasoning and emotion behind my chosen color palette for painting. And don't forget the buffet thing. They all liked and disliked the same foods as Charlie and I do."

"Don't get paranoid, Emmaline. I'll find out what's up for you." Jensen consoled.

"Just tell them that too, please Jensen."

"I agree," said Charlie. "They understood my answers like it reinforced something they already knew. I got the idea they only asked to get confirmation of our identification with each other."

Jensen looked perplexed. "Okay, you guys, I'll let them know your theory. I-yi-yi. But can I tell them you'll do the seminars?"

They looked at each other and found no protest. "Double time for all hours we stay, even asleep," Emmaline threw into the ring. "And the classes are to be two and a half hours max. I can't fill more time than that with so little prep."

"I think they'll go for it. Just make sure you pull together a presentation for the seminar that does us proud. I know you will. First one will start at ten a.m. And don't forget the lounge appearance tonight." Jensen left them with a wave of confidence.

When Charlie and Emmaline passed through the lobby to go out for a cab, almost everyone lit up as they saw them. Many nodded or waved, but they didn't mob them again. Emmaline shivered. That was just how she would greet an acquaintance or acknowledge someone she admired. She would let them know she knew them but not intrude.

The cabby looked at them indifferently. "Isadora's," Charlie directed. And the two sunk back in their seats. The stars had receded from supergiant to black dwarf status.

= FIFTEEN =

Emmaline knocked on Charlie's door for the third time. Just as she turned to go back and try the phone, he surfaced peering through a small crack. He swung the door wide when he spotted her.

"Oh, Emmaline, are we going somewhere?" he yawned. He was astounded at how great she looked. No artsy silk skirt this time. She was all-out cocktail finery. Black halter dress with just the slightest silver shimmer. He dropped his eyes to see her four inch heels. He refrained from a quip about whether she could walk in them, remembering her grace the night before.

"Our late night lounge appearance, remember? Well, obviously not, but can you pull it together?" Her tone was harsh.

"Wow, you're going to be a hard date to live up to," he said. Emmaline actually blushed.

She softened. "You're gorgeous, Charlie. Just wash the sleep out of your eyes, put on your cocktail hour suit, and slick back that endearing cowlick." She smirked, her diamond eyes a-twinkle.

"Gimme fifteen minutes," he pleaded.

"Must be nice to be a guy," she turned away down the hall. It had taken her two hours to look like a sophisticated woman.

He wasted ten of his seconds watching her walk very capably away.

=

Charlie stuck out his elbow as they approached the hotel's Gemini Room, and Emmaline grabbed hold to be escorted in. She was extra-nervous after their strange afternoon, and more than a little over-tired. She envied Charlie's ability to nap. She would've been a loggy-groggy mess if she had slept. He looked fresh as an alpine peak. Downright handsome, now that she noticed.

The room broke into applause as they entered. Charlie and Emmaline glanced at each other ruefully and turned with gracious smiles to their adoring fans. The bartender waved them over to the VIP table when he realized the size of their forming entourage. Emmaline slid around into the elevated round booth. Charlie joined her but stayed close to the outside edge. The group surrounded them, able to get close enough to talk without crowding them. Charlie eased into the comfort of the booth a little.

A bright-eyed young woman set a gin and tonic at Emmaline's elbow. "It's Tanqueray. I thought you'd like it." The woman smiled and raised her brows. Emmaline was pleased - it was her favorite drink. Even an extra lime. That was eerie.

A young dark-haired man shifted the skinny tie on his immaculate retro suit, and bent forward to deliver a Chai Tea, extra-tall to Charlie. Though Charlie didn't frequent latte stands, he always got a Chai when someone insisted on ordering him something. Very few people drank it as this one was delivered - with only hot water and no milk. Charlie did. He nodded thanks for the gift to the guy whose suit so resembled his own. "Nice tie," he offered.

"Thanks, I just got it this afternoon," the guy said. He backed off - nonchalant.

"Figures," mumbled Charlie.

Emmaline was busy with her own group of admirers and didn't have time to contemplate the gaggle of Charlie clones. After complimenting four of the women on their dresses, it occurred to her that something was very wrong. She hated cocktail dresses for the most part. There were a select few that she thought had enough personality without being trampy.

Yet when she looked around the room, she liked about three-quarters of them, and they were all on her groupies.

She changed her conversation from compliments to questions, "So where did you get that lovely dress?"

Without fail the answer told it was purchased that afternoon. Since they had first seen Emmaline. She looked up at the men in the room - and Charlie - it was obvious.

She knew they needed to get a hold of Jensen, quick. There was something terribly wrong with the drug they'd so generously distributed to the populous. And the ramifications of what they'd done were unknown, but so far it was giving Emmaline the absolute heebie-jeebies. She looked across at Charlie who, to her surprise, was laughing and seemed to be having a great time. He was withdrawn at work parties, and she had never seen him in a bar, only heard him bemoan the times he was forced into hanging out there with some friend or family member.

"You know The Enigmas?!" she heard him exclaim in a very un-Charlie-like shriek.

"Yeah, I just looked them up this afternoon. I was intrigued after our conversation about the Vancouver wave-punk scene, and I spent the day surfing the web pulling out all kinds of gems. I can't believe I never noticed them before," she heard one guy say.

She then realized that shriek may have been the most Charlie-like thing she had ever heard. He was in his glory. Surrounded by his own. Which, now that she thought about it, was unusual for him since he was so unusual.

She glanced at the Astrological themed clock at the end of the bar. They were in the Age of Charlarius, and it was only eleven. There was no escape until at least midnight, and they should work it through until one. Calling Jensen would have to wait. There was no way she could hear to make a call in here. She took small comfort as she remembered he promised to let corporate know about the afternoon's events. Their commercials had already run their course for the night and weren't scheduled for airing again until prime time the next evening. And the product couldn't be pulled from store shelves tonight either. She'd let Charlie have his fun.

"Emmaline...Emmaline?" she heard as she turned back to the gals.

"Oh, sorry, I got distracted thinking about something. What were you saying?"

"Oh don't you hate it when that happens? I've been doing that all day," the girl agreed.

"Actually I love it when that happens." Emmaline was obstinate.

"Well, yeah, it's fun while your mind is gone, but it's kind of tough when you come back to reality and the person you're with gives you grief."

The other women laughed heartily. Not one genteel tee-hee in the bunch. Emmaline had always been proud of her uninhibited laughter. Hearing it echo back at her grilled her psyche. It made no statement when all the girls did it. It was just loud. She missed Jen's little giggle and gregarious ease. There wasn't a flirty-girl in the place.

"What's wrong, Emmaline? You look peevish," another woman asked. Her dirty-blonde bob created an odd triangle as she tipped her head in concern.

"What's your name?" Emmaline tried. Maybe she could get them to remember their own identities.

"I'm Jayna Pritchet. Nice to meet you, Emmaline," she reported without a blink.

"Where are you from Jayna?"

"I'm from Iowa, but I might move out to the coast. The area I come from is so limited in ethnicity and diversity. I'm interested in the varied cultural expression and artistic freedom in the West." Her words were ironic among the enthusiastic nods of twenty Emmaline-like 'individuals'.

"And I am Greta Parsons. I am so excited to meet a painter like you, Emmaline." She had an interesting accent, perhaps influenced by German? But that wasn't quite it. "I have been wandering the streets all afternoon in an ecstasy of color and light. When you spoke about your work in answer to my question earlier today, I could feel the intensity of the play of colors, one with another, and my creative self came bursting into bloom."

"Until today I never realized the richness of a life where everything is viewed as an opportunity to create," another gal chimed in – an unmistakable Brit. "When you were on stage, the inspiration welled up inside me until I finally understood. My sister is an artist, and I always tell her to ease up on the crazy stuff. It's not crazy. I'd be crazy to put it down. I see!" The third woman's bouncing red curls accented her enthusiasm.

This was too much. Emmaline needed an out. "Uh, hello there," she called to one of the guys in desperation, "Are you from the U.S.? West coast perhaps?"

"Well, yes, actually…" he looked back and forth at his shoes and returned to his conversation with another pseudo-Charlie.

"I'd like you to meet Jayna," she insisted.

"…like when you come out of the trees and…What?" he acknowledged.

"Jayna. She's from Iowa, and she's interested in west coast diversity. Why don't you fill her in."

"Hi, I'm Emmaline," she got up and leaned across the table with her hand extended to one of the younger guys.

"Steve," he shook her hand dutifully and withdrew.

He couldn't get away that easily. "Where are you from, Steve?"

"I'm from Portland."

"Oh, another west coast guy. Do you climb?"

"Not yet, but I was checking out trails and peaks all day on the web. There're so many things I haven't seen. Charlie was just giving me pointers…"

"I'll bet there are some beautiful places. The forest greens and glacial blues. Meet Greta and um…"

"Beatrice," the British red-head chimed in.

"We were just talking about the beauty in the world and all the wonderful colors." Emmaline led.

"Oh, yes, the natural beauty is overwhelming in the western States. Much like the Lake District back home. And I never realized until today how everything can be broken down into such sleek shapes." Beatrice took the bait.

"And the colors blend or accent the shapes. What peaks did you see online today?" Greta continued.

It was working. Emmaline escaped from the booth and began to mix with the group of Charlies. One by one she engaged them in conversation with the ladies until she had slipped the women completely. Peace at last!

The real Charlie was still caught up in rapturous conversation about the pros and cons of Sci Fi writers with his only fan not talking to the semi-Emmalines.

"Hi, I'm Emmaline Kinner," she demanded of his captivated pseudo-Charlie.

"I'm Fred Benner. From Idaho."

"Glad to meet you, Fred. Um, can I talk to Charlie for a minute? I'd like you to meet Greta." She grabbed his elbow and marched him over to join the group, then made a quick retreat.

"Charlie!" she stage-whispered. "What's going on here?" She pulled him over to the end of the bar.

"Yeah, it's weird, huh? It's gotta be the drug, but it's kinda funny."

"Funny?! You think this is funny? That's bullshit! It's the creepiest, most bizarre thing that's ever happened to me - and I've been through some winners before."

"Calm down, Emmaline. You look like you're about to bust a vessel in your forehead."

"Yeah, I better watch what the hell I'm doing; I might cause all the women to bleed to death. They'll probably slash their foreheads open to be more like me," she flipped.

"Oh come on. It's not that bad," he soothed. "They're not really you. They're just interested in the same things as you are."

"But they have my sensibilities. They understand art." She had actually whined.

He winced. "So? I think you're over-reacting." He eased up when frustration puckered her brow. "Besides, we've only got another hour, and we can't do anything till tomorrow. I know you've worked that out too." He gave his crooked smile. "Have some fun with it. When will you ever get to hang out with this many people that appreciate what you appreciate?"

"Sorry, Charlie." She answered his grin with a forlorn smirk. "I just don't groove on that like you do. I'm me, they're not."

"Okay, sorry, Emmaline. I'm having a good time, and I'm going back to my minions." He raised one brow and flashed another cockeyed smile as he left her at the bar and joined the fray.

= SIXTEEN =

Emmaline ordered another Tanq-and-Tonic and was somewhat soothed as Bob Marley began to play on the sound system. She relaxed into the reggae beat and created a strategy to survive the lunacy. She gathered herself and decided to grill them. But she was almost undone when she turned from the bar to a scene of women bobbing to the reggae. "Steady, Kinner," she mumbled to herself.

"So, Greta, have you ever done any artwork before?" she threw out into the crowd.

"Not yet, but I feel so inspired," she looked vibrant.

"What's your idea for an art piece?" The others tuned in when Emmaline asked the question with all of her presentation gusto. She thought it might put the woman on the spot and expose her as the fraud she was.

"I was out at lunch today in the café down the street sitting by the window. The passersby were wearing a wide palette of colors, and as the famous Chicago wind blew their scarves and coats, and the garbage blew along with them, I saw the scene as a flowing stream. A river of hues running in a multi-textured rush of life. Beauty and filth woven together in one billowing scarf of humanity and its swirling debris."

Emmaline's brow was up. Her lips folded inward. The woman actually had artistic vision.

"Oh, that's lovely!" Beatrice shared, "while you sat and watched the movement of the streets, I walked. And instead of evaluating the people I passed, I was taken with the sky and the forms in the city. The play of light on the buildings, reflecting on the geometric space of the windows. The perspective as I looked up the building surface, and the distortion of the city's reflections. And what captivated me most were all the facets of the color grey. And then the sun broke through and the most delicious gold and light emerald green contrasted the grey. And the flash of the sun's beam...it left me breathless. I merely wanted to paint. I wished I could leave the conference, but I have a job to do. So I decided I would come and let you know what you helped me see, Emmaline. I have never had such an experience in all my life."

"Well, that's really great, Beatrice..."

"Oh, please call me Bea," she pleaded.

"Bea. But doesn't it seem strange to you that both you and Greta suddenly have eyes to see?"

"Oh, no, not at all. We were talking about that before you and Charlie arrived," Bea continued. "We all feel as though we've connected with our actual selves, and it seems like it started during your presentation today."

"Yes, that's exactly what I mean." Emmaline's insistent tone again grabbed the attention of the larger group. "I think you're just imitating me because of the drug sample you took. You think you're me."

Bea's brows drew in, and Greta spoke up again. "I don't think I am you at all. I feel aware of myself in a way I have never been before. I am definitely me. I'm just a far more dynamic and creative me, because I became conscious of what's around me. This afternoon I didn't worry about what was expected of me. I just explored. And what I found was myself. I feel more at ease than I ever have in my life. Do you feel like that, Emmaline?"

"Well, yeah, most of the time. I have my moments of social discomfort, but they're rare and fleeting. It's usually when I'm presenting a precarious ad concept, or if I submit an art portfolio to be juried or something."

"That sounds like a small dose of self-doubt," Jayna volunteered. "That's different than not knowing yourself or squelching your self-expression. I'll bet you have the most incredible clothes at home. I like your dress tonight, but this isn't your preferred type of clothing is it? You're probably a mass of color and pattern most the time - with a wrap of black?"

Emmaline nodded. She thought a moment. "Hey, Charlie?"

He looked up from his conversation with a smile still lining his features.

"Do these guys know what they're talking about, or are they just mirroring you?"

"What kind of question is that, Emmaline?" Charlie smirked. "Nice."

"I think we should all look at what happened today. Those of you who have come to see Charlie and me again, seem to look like us and think like us. You have said yourselves that you see and feel different today than you ever have before."

"But none of these guys are Charlie." Charlie retorted. "And they came in the way they are. They didn't study me and copy-cat it. James is definitely James. While we can see eye to eye - which I admit is somewhat rare for me - he has original ideas. As original as my own. That's what's so fascinating."

"No lie," confirmed James. "I think I just found the parts of myself that are in line with Charlie. It's kind of like I'm bending toward his center. But I'm not Charlie."

"And I don't think I look like you, Emmaline," Greta reconfirmed. "Would that I could." She flicked her brows flirtatiously and the depth of the creases in her forehead contrasted noticeably to Emmaline's.

"I don't mean it literally. But when you look around the room. Don't you see a bunch of Charlies?" Emmaline tried.

"There are an atypical number of retro suits," Jayna admitted.

"But as Charlie pointed out, these men came here this way, and they had never seen how Charlie dresses other than the climbing gear he was wearing earlier. They have their own minds. They just have Charlie's taste."

"How many of you bought what you're wearing today?" Emmaline insisted.

Twenty-three of the thirty or so fans raised their hand.

"And that doesn't disturb anyone but me?" She crossed her arms and cocked her head along with one brow.

"We are on holiday here. It's natural we should shop," Greta countered.

"Does your new outfit resemble the clothing you brought to wear?"

"I suppose you've got me there. This dress has much more life than my old brown one. But I hadn't thought about what I was wearing lately - before today. I'm not so sure my taste has changed, I just bothered to consult my preference and mood when I was at the store."

"So you're saying you are wearing what feels right?"

"Yes, that's it!" Greta agreed.

"I rest my case!" Emmaline shouted, slapping a nearby table with her hand. "When we were trying to define my style for our ad campaign, that was exactly how I described it."

"But I am wearing what feels right to me, not to you." Greta looked shaken.

"It feels right to me too though," Emmaline's brow furrowed. "I've never liked so many outfits in one bar in my life. It's creeping me out. I'm used to being - different."

"Chill, Emmaline," Charlie put in. "These women were inspired by your artistic character to look inward at their own more expressive and creative desires. What's so disturbing about that?"

"Their desires and expressions are the same as mine," Emmaline demanded. "That's not normal!"

"They all look normal to me. How 'bout to you guys?" Charlie waved his finger at the pseudo-Charlies.

"Great," agreed Fred. "Downright glamorous."

"You look maaahvalous, dahling," James said mocking Emmaline with a cocked brow.

"See! Charlie! You did that just like, Charlie!"

"Sarcasm is universal, Emmaline. It's 'the norm.'" Charlie clinched his argument between his quote-gesturing fingers.

"Actually," James' face drew in, "it's not like me."

Everyone grew quiet. A man outside their group cackled oddly at the bar.

"I'm dry as a board. I don't clown or tease or feign dramatic accents," he admitted.

"Hmm." Charlie wondered out loud. "Why not?"

"Usually I can't think of anything fast enough, and when I do, I don't speak up. I suppose because I don't want to hurt anyone's feelings, and I don't like it if people misunderstand my intent."

"I have bullet-train-worthy wit speed, and I'm not afraid to use it," Charlie quipped.

"When you're among friends," Emmaline pointed out.

"True." Charlie scratched his cowlick and thought a moment. "Your reasons for holding back are similar to mine when I become quiet. And if the drug did what it was supposed to do, it would've made you feel more comfortable and helped you relate to those around you. Maybe this evening is just a matter of removed inhibition."

"So if we were free to be ourselves, we would all be Charlie and Emmaline?" Fred concluded with blatant doubt.

The party was dampened. The camaraderie of common interests was washed away in uncertainty.

"I think I will be going for the night," Greta announced.

"That's just what I was about to say," Beatrice said with worry.

"I think that's a normal response when the party wanes," said Emmaline. "We don't need to get paranoid."

The women smiled and pulled away from each other.

"Are any of you signed up for my class tomorrow?" Emmaline called before they had made it out of the room.

All of the women turned back toward her and answered in unison. "I am." They laughed awkwardly as they continued to move to the door.

"That's disturbing," Emmaline mumbled as she waved goodnight. "See you tomorrow, ladies," she called after them.

Charlie traded a few more ideas with Fred and James and the other guys as they left.

Emmaline headed for the door as well. "Good night, Charlie." She waved.

"Not so fast, Missy," he strode across the floor to her side. "Can I escort you back to your door, Ma'am?"

"Uh, sure, whatever, Charlie." She took his offered elbow and walked with him.

"Boy, you really know how to kick a guy in the nuts," he mock-pouted.

"Quit clowning around. This is serious."

"How is it serious?" he asked as he pushed the elevator button. "I mean, I agree that we need to let corporate know about our rather different - or should I say clone-like - evening, but drugs wear off, right? Even if it really was something mind-bending, it'll be over tomorrow."

"It stays in your system for seventy-two hours," Emmaline recited, remembering the product data she used in the ad copy.

"It's an expression, Emmaline. Remember expression? That's supposed to be the essence of you." They stepped off the elevator into the hall.

"I just hope it quits being the essence of everyone else sooner rather than later."

"We'll call Joe first thing in the morning - after we sleep in - and everything will be fine. Truly, Emmaline. You just need to ease up. There's nothing we can do anyway."

"I don't believe in, 'nothing we can do.'"

"Well, you're right. We can go to that wonderful, fabulous place called, 'bed.'"

She rolled her eyes, pulled out her card key and pulled her hand from Charlie's elbow. "Goodnight, Charlie."

"It certainly was." He got no smile from her. "Goodnight, Emmaline. The world could do with more women like you."

The corners of her mouth crimped upward despite her best efforts. "Thanks, Charlie. It wasn't so bad having more guys like you around either." She slipped inside her room and kicked her shoes off by the door. It felt wonderful to be her own person at last.

.

= SEVENTEEN =

Emmaline waited as long as she could but at seven-thirty had to ring the phone for Charlie. Preparation time for their class was zipping away. She had puzzled an outline together in her head as she was moving from sleep into waking. During that time her associative sense was strong and images flowed without regard for convention. Then the ideas and visions whirled into a linear whole and she knew it was time to get up and write.

The line went to voicemail. She hung up and rang again.

Charlie groaned and rolled in the almost made up bed. He had slept like the proverbial log. And he was still doing so when this infernal ringtone forced itself upon his consciousness over and over and... "Hello," he muddled into his phone.

"Good morning, Sunshine," Emmaline cooed. She waited - giving him room to be Charlie.

"The Sun hasn't risen yet," he finally managed.

"Ah, but the day has begun," she lamented. "I have our class presentation roughed out, but I need to brief you and polish it up."

"Okay," he grunted as he moved to a sitting position, pulling the now mussed blue covers around him. "I'll polish up my briefs and don them for the party. Perhaps I best put on the remainder of my clothing as well. Shall I knock at your room?"

"Sure. How long?" Her tone said minimum needed.

"Twenty minutes?"

"Go to it, dude. We'll discuss the class over breakfast in the Palm Room." She smiled.

=

When the knock came, she closed her laptop and gathered the items she had put into her 'take with you' spot since she got in last evening - or rather that morning.

"Hi, Bright-eyes," she greeted as she came out of the room tucking her card key into an inner pocket of her purse.

"Uh, good morning, Emmaline. You look like you were expecting someone."

"Oh, Jensen!" she jumped in surprise. "Uh, Charlie is meeting me to go over our class."

"Good, very good. I just need to have a few words with you kids to fill you in on my call with corporate."

"Oh, so you talked to them already. Thank God for that. Are they pulling the drug?"

"Pulling it?" he looked confused. "Why would they be pulling it?"

"Because of all the weirdness yesterday. Although I guess you don't know how strange it got once we reached the Gemini Room."

"Were there new developments?" he asked as they moved toward Charlie's room.

"Well, I guess just a deepening of the same really. It seemed like the whole bar was full of Charlies and Emmalines. By the end of the evening, we were even discussing it with all of them."

"Oh dear," his brows drew down.

"I know," she agreed. "It's got to be stopped."

"No, I mean it may be unfortunate that you pointed it out to them."

They arrived near Charlie's door. Emmaline hesitated and stepped back hoping to give Charlie time to come out at his own pace. "Well, they need to know if they're not themselves, don't they?"

"Well, Emmaline, that's what…" he was interrupted by Charlie's door swinging open.

His eyes took in the two of them, and he greeted them like he'd expected both all along. "Good morning, comrades."

"Hi, Charlie," Jensen said with good cheer.

Emmaline smiled with resignation.

"I talked to corporate, and I need to talk to you guys about today," Jensen caught him up. "May I join you for breakfast?"

"Yes, of course," Emmaline replied formally.

"Okay then, but we should leave the hotel. This is somewhat confidential."

"I better dip back in for my coat." Charlie turned.

"We'll meet you back in the hall," Emmaline said as she headed back for hers too. She shivered.

=

They blew in off the street, entering a hole-in-the-wall bagel place that advertised a two-egg special. Jensen said it looked greasy enough to ward off most other conference attendees, but Emmaline just hoped it wouldn't ward off the stability of her stomach for the day. Charlie was not yet awake enough to have an opinion.

They ordered from the skinny, disheveled young man behind the counter and took their choice of the many empty tables. Jensen sat them in the corner farthest from the hired help. Charlie lounged, and Emmaline sat forward - ready for the scoop.

Jensen dove right in. "So here's the thing. I had a conference call with the Top office, and they were surprised to hear of the mass enthusiasm for the campaign. When I explained the intensity of the identification between the audience and you - like with the food - and the high number that came to the green room, they were amazed. Apparently nothing like this was picked up in the studies. After mulling it over, we surmised it's because of the relative isolation of the subjects from one another in the trials. The situations and the people they were surrounded by when they took *Assimilaire* were all different from each other. Also, their experiences were reported back to us by the subjects. Here, we have the reports of…the objects, if you will. It never occurred to the clinicians to interview the people from the groups in which the study subjects placed themselves to measure their comfort or experience. So if this type of mirroring of characteristics did happen, there was no one who recognized it. No platter of pickled beets to shine light on the situation."

"Oh, but Jensen, it got so much worse." Emmaline couldn't contain herself. "They dressed like us without ever seeing our eveningwear, and they created new ideas using our sensibilities. It was as if they thought with our minds and saw with our eyes. It was surreal - nightmarish."

"Surely you're exaggerating, Emmaline. You do tend to be dramatic."

Charlie smirked but then supported her. "I have to admit, there's something to what she's saying. I wasn't as disturbed as she was, but it was very noticeable, and the similarities ran deep."

"Interesting. Interesting." Jensen was lost in thought for a moment. "Was anyone unhappy or having ill effects?"

"No one besides, Emmaline, and she just didn't like everyone stealing her thunder," Charlie teased.

"So everyone seemed safe and well?"

"I suppose," she admitted, "if it's well to be someone other than yourself."

"What happened when you discussed it with them?" Jensen tented his fingers.

"More like confronted them," Charlie replied. "Emmaline just couldn't let it go. But they took it pretty well. Most of them defended their behavior as being their own. They said they felt as though they were tuned in to their real selves or parts of themselves they'd been afraid to express. They claimed they were inspired by our freedom to be individuals."

"Yes, but when we showed them by example how closely their 'real selves' shadowed us, some of them grew uncomfortable," she added.

"Did the evening end badly?" Jensen looked concerned.

"It got a little strained near the end, but I think everyone left feeling fine," Charlie assessed.

"Yeah," she agreed, "I think we raised some doubt, but they were pretty unquenchable."

"Hmm." It was unclear whether the lines in Jensen's face deepened in worry for the crowd or worry for what he came to tell them. "I wish you hadn't created consciousness of the issue, but I think it will still work."

"What will still work?" Emmaline jumped right in.

Jensen's eyes shot to the scraggy guy who was bringing their meals. The waiter looked oblivious to everything including their conversation. They were silent till he withdrew.

"Corporate sees this as a great, semi-controlled environment to see how the situation plays out. There are two more days at the conference to study the subjects that were dosed at the kick-off presentation. We'll continue to give out more of the medication and track what occurs," he finally answered.

"They want to use them as guinea pigs?" Emmaline spurted.

The listless counter guy's head pivoted in her direction. She hushed her mouth, sat back and stuffed some scrambled eggs in it. Her stomach was doomed.

"Now that's definitely over-dramatic," Jensen cautioned. "They took the medication willingly, and just because it's having unexpected effects doesn't mean it's harmful in any way. It's not a calculated experiment. We aren't trapping them or tricking them. We simply want to take advantage of this naturally occurring observation opportunity."

"I'm not sure it's natural at all," she worried.

"You work for a pharmaceutical company, Emmaline. Our industry is based on tweaking and manipulating what's natural, for a supernatural result - healing. We told them it would change their reality. They accepted that. And it will wear off eventually. We're just asking that you watch what happens until it does. I'll be staying to observe also, and I'll be talking to the folks from Product Development that stayed the night. We'll spend most of the day at

The Wickham with the vendors since you'll be here at The Milieu. Just go teach your classes today. No problem."

"I believe you said something about handing out more of the medication." Charlie remembered.

"Well yes, we have more samples for you to distribute at the beginning of your classes, and we'd like you to use your creative persuasion to get them to take it."

"No." Emmaline's mouth imitated her name.

"No?" Jensen was taken aback. "I don't think it's considered optional," he pushed. "I'm to pick up the additional samples from the Product guys by nine and bring it to your conference room for distribution. Why would you say no?"

"I just don't feel good about this," she insisted.

"Do you feel the same, Charlie?" he asked.

"Well, I won't refuse, but I do feel uncomfortable giving out more of it when we don't understand what's really going on here."

"Let's review," Jensen suggested. "People took the drug and became a big happy group of people. Those who talked to you reported feeling inspired and wonderful. The worst thing that's been observed is the way they were inspired was more similar to each other than we'd come to expect from other testing. The problem with this is....what?"

"It doesn't seem like it would be a big deal to let it go on for a couple more days, Emmaline," Charlie agreed with Jensen.

"And you're sure the effects will wear off?" she hung on to her skepticism.

"One of the things Product Development makes sure of is there's soon no trace of it in the subject's system. The idea is to get them to buy more. And I'm sure we would've seen side effects reported if it lingered."

"What about long term psychological effects?" she pushed.

"There was a slight improvement in confidence and lessening of social anxiety over the long term studies, but no one showed signs on their tests of gaining someone else's personality, if that's what you're asking."

"Perhaps because we didn't know who they were mirroring, like you said."

"And?"

"And I guess it's not worth losing my job over as long as the effect is temporary," she conceded.

Charlie set to eating his rather puny bagel and cream cheese - the matter settled.

"We need to go over our presentation!" she exclaimed, looking at the time on her cell.

"Okay," Jensen hopped up from the table. "I'll leave you kids to work that out on your own. See you just before ten at the Hemlock room."

= EIGHTEEN =

Emmaline was checking the class notes on her laptop in their conference room and fretting about last minute details, when Jensen and Calvin, Jason and Ronny from the crew came in with boxes of samples. Her face puckered like she had swallowed a moldy frog.

"Isn't that a lot of boxes?" she frowned.

"We were hoping you could entice them to take a few to continue using or distribute to friends," he replied.

"Nice," she mumbled. She glanced over at Charlie who was following the crew with his eyes through a glaze of personal iPod-bubble. She waved her hands, crisscrossing them to call him in for a landing.

He looked up at the clock and pulled the buds from his ears. "What, Emmaline? Do you need me before class time?"

"I'm feeling a bit shaky, and I thought talking things through with you might help." Her greasy stomach was doing flip-flops.

"Go," he was amiable.

"See you later, Jensen," she saluted hoping to get-him-gone.

"Okay, kids, you're on your own. You're to wrap up by twelve-thirty. I'll have Calvin and the guys come back by to pick up left over product after the three to five-thirty session." He walked out at last.

"So we have two sessions to drug up as many people as we can. Shit." She groaned.

"Is that what you're worried about? I thought you were having trouble with the class content."

"You know me, Charlie, I can present in my sleep. In fact I made up the entire presentation while halfway in dreamland this morning. Piece o' cake. But I still haven't come to terms with this whole medicating my students thing."

"But you agreed to do it this morning."

"Yeah, and now I feel jammed into it. I still don't feel good at all."

"Remember it will wear off. Plus if there was anything really bad, it would've shown up somewhere in the studies. Right? I think it's just nerves."

"Exaustion. Yeah, I can relate to that. Maybe that's what's making my hands wobble."

"I'm just scared to death of giving my part of the class," he admitted.

"Don't worry, Igor, we'll just drug them before you go on stage. You'll be Charlie-who-can-do-no-wrong." She smiled a broad one.

He responded to the twinkle in her eye. "That's one way for me to hold a crowd." He cocked his eyebrow and grinned his sideways grin.

The first of their students entered the room, and they quieted down. She was middle-aged with wild, curly grey-streaked hair. She wore a vivid, hand-painted silk scarf with her simple black cardigan and tank. Her eyes flashed at them with energy and interest, but she kept to herself.

After five minutes the room was almost filled. There was an inordinate amount of artsy women and geeky men for the average group, but nothing as odd looking as the group last night in the Gemini room. It was crowded and a good thing they had another session to accommodate everyone. Charlie paced around and poured himself a glass of ice water from a pitcher in the corner. Emmaline busied herself fussing with the laptop whether she needed to or not. Charlie looked at her and then at the clock, catching her eye. She nodded.

"Good morning, everyone," she began. "We're so glad you can join us for Marketing a Successful Life. When I contemplated this class title that was prescribed for us, I was inclined to break it into three sections. Marketing, Successful, and Life. With our company's new product *Assimilaire*, the three have been united in an unusual way. Perhaps this is one reason the campaign resonated with so many." She paused. "For those who may not know, *Assimilaire* is a breakthrough product that reduces social anxiety by providing a feeling of identification with those around which brings a sense of acceptance and well-being." She smiled at the nodding heads around the room.

Emmaline caught her breath as she saw, not one but two women scoop their cappuccino foam out of their cup and lick it from their finger - just as she would do. She struggled back to the agenda.

"Before our class officially begins, I, Emmaline Kinner, and my colleague, Charlie Simon would like to welcome you to enjoy a sample of *Assimilaire*, if you're interested." She gestured to the table near the water station. "You're also encouraged to take extra samples for later or to give it to your friends to try. Please leave your seats and help yourself to these now." She secretly hoped many would stay seated, but everyone in the room took the offering and drank the Kool-Aid.

Emmaline was taken aback yet again when she recognized Marilyn Jennings. It had taken time looking at this group to discover the blonde beauty that had stood out so sharply at their evening meeting with Joe. Her hair was ruffled and her dress so relaxed it was next to impossible to visualize her in the chic green number she'd worn when they met. Emmaline looked again just to be sure it was the same woman. It was Marilyn alright, but the jury was out on 'same'.

When the class was seated again, Emmaline cleared her throat, "Now why did every one of you try this product right now?" She avoided Marilyn's eye and pointed to a woman dressed in a practical black wool skirt and tights topped by a deep jewel tone sweater with a loose pattern woven into it.

"I took some yesterday at the kick-off, and I felt a great sense of well-being ever since. I came here to find out more about the product and how you put together the marketing campaign."

"So you took it after having a good experience the first time," Emmaline summarized.

The woman nodded.

"Did anyone take it for the first time just now?" Emmaline asked.

She scanned the room for a volunteer and coughed, choking on her surprise. Sharon Green was in attendance too - well, in a manner of speaking. The shrewd, keen eyes that cut through everything at their dinner meeting were glued to a notebook filled with textured paper where she was doodling away. And her shoes were pictures of practicality. No enviable Corinthian leather here. They looked like they'd fit right in with the ones tumbled around the door of Emmaline's apartment.

A young man in a meticulous, modern suit waved his hand with a big 'hello' to her attention.

She snapped back to presentation mode. "So what made you take the sample?" she asked him.

"Well, I assumed it would be helpful to know something firsthand about the product you're going to speak about. I also felt a bit nervous with this many people in the room and thought it might help me relax."

"So you were researching the product. Perhaps curious about it? And you were interested in the product's effect as being helpful to you. Is that a fair recounting?"

"Yes," he agreed.

"So in the realm of Marketing, I did well to introduce the product in a way that made you interested and curious to know more. And it was also germane to your decision to try it, that the product offered something you desired. You wanted to feel more at ease. It claims to make you feel more at ease."

"What specifically brought you to the class?" she aimed at the same guy.

"I heard it was a big sensation at the kick-off yesterday, which unfortunately I had to miss."

"Word of mouth. Reputation. Buzz. Good."

"And now that you've tried it, did it fit your expectation?"

She saw him go inward before he replied, "Well, I'm talking in front of a group of people I felt smothered by when I walked in. And I feel some of the energy alluded to by my friends who attended the kick-off. Yes, it seems to be what I believed it would be."

"So the product delivers the things that were in the ads and in the buzz you heard. I'll say the key word again. It Delivers.

She continued. "Marketing boils down to this. To find what's desirable in the product. To spin that point in a way that piques interest. And to make sure the product can deliver it. It's not a great mystery, but it can be tricky to find that essence and communicate it well."

"Let's move on for a moment to the second word, Successful. What makes something successful?"

A young woman covered in various plaids shot her hand into the air. "Achieving your objective."

"Yes, excellent," Emmaline complimented, realizing it was exactly what she would say. "So let's break that down. Achieving implies doing - moving forward. And reaching the goal or objective only brings real success if it's a good goal. We're back to determining the essence."

"And Life. I at first wondered what life had to do with Marketing and Success. Everything of course. You must use your life experience to recognize the essence of a product and to convey it in a creative, interesting way. Also, it's very important to Marketing Success and Success in general for there to be Life in what you do. The campaign must breathe. If it's toxic to the imagination or doesn't circulate well, it'll fall dead at your feet."

The women in the class laughed heartily. More than one man cocked an eyebrow.

"And of course there's the Life that surges in you when you see the success of a marketing campaign you've launched." She glowed as she moved toward her conclusion. "So you see Marketing a Successful Life is an inter-dependent concept. You must have life to succeed in marketing and your marketing success will add to your life. Any questions?"

A rather Charlie-like fellow looked up for acknowledgement.

"Yes?" she encouraged.

"Well, I thought this class was going to focus more on what a successful life is. Yesterday when I saw your presentation, I was amazed by how original and unique both you and Charlie are. The commercials are appealing because the people that usually intimidate me become wonderful like you. It's the ultimate success to win people over that way. You of course do it through marketing, because that's your job, but the class title implied you might give insight on how to do it in life."

Emmaline hesitated. "Well…" she bought some time, "I think we're back to your life being the source of your inspiration. Your experiences should pave the way for you to connect with your surroundings and with other people. It should give you tools to distill things down to their essence and form objectives you can move toward."

"Well, I can see how that applies to life. But I've never been very good at using my experience or feeling connected to others. I felt these things for the first time yesterday when I saw your presentation. I really feel in tune with you - especially with Charlie. I just want to learn more."

Emmaline grew uncomfortable. "Charlie, I believe you have some things to add to the presentation." She gave him the floor.

"Uh, yes, I'm not sure if it will be 'the essence of what you desire,'" he said to the young man and elicited a shared grin, "but I do have a few things to say. One, is when you're working out a campaign for marketing or for life, it's important to maintain your individual perspective. You need to be aware of your unique contribution to the whole. I think that's much of what made the campaign for *Assimilaire* intriguing. Since the idea for the logo came to me from something I'm personally interested in - Incan stonework - it was uniquely mine. I'm fascinated how they used individually shaped stones and placed them together in the way they fit best with each other. They honed their edges but took them as they were and used each one's natural character to make the strongest whole. Likewise, it's important for you to see who you are and where you fit, instead of trying to put your square self into a round hole."

"I completely understand," a woman in the back row burst out. "I'm so glad I came here today. For the first time, I feel like I can make a difference. I can see things in myself that might contribute to a greater whole. Usually, I just try to follow the norm. In my job I always present what's safe or what I think will fit best with what my boss is looking for. Now I see it's my unique ideas that have the most potential. And oddly enough, that makes me feel more unified with all of you instead of alienated like I usually feel."

"Exactly," the guy next to her agreed. "Thinking about the essence of things, I realize my ideas are worthwhile. I usually sublimate them to what others suggest. Now I feel bolder. I think I'll be able to speak up for myself at the next meeting."

"And I just feel so creative!" another woman exclaimed. "I usually have trouble coming up with ideas. I'm not sure I've ever found the essence of anything before. But now when I look around the room, I feel like my eyes have a different way of seeing. This has been very enlightening."

Emmaline looked at Charlie. He met her gaze. It was happening again.

"How many of you were at the kick-off?" Charlie asked.

At least three quarters of the class raised their hands.

"And how many of you tried *Assimilaire* yesterday?"

Almost all of the same people raised their hands. Charlie recognized Steve and Fred from the bar, and then noticed that Jayna was also in the class.

"And you all wanted to try the product again today?"

"I don't know why anyone wouldn't," Jayna volunteered. "We've been assured over and over it has no side effects and is non-addictive. And while I didn't feel driven to have more, I really enjoyed the sense of depth and well-being I got yesterday. I wanted to feel that way again, and I must admit I'm curious if the effect is cumulative - if I might feel even more wonderful today?"

"I know it's not the point of the class," Emmaline put in, "but I'm curious too. We were saying the product must deliver as promised. I'd say it's a good sign, and actually incredible that all of you tried it again. So does it have a cumulative effect, may I ask?" she looked at Jayna.

"I don't think so, or not exactly. It could be building up, I guess, but it feels about the same as yesterday only more comfortable and familiar. But that's what's so fascinating about it. I feel like I'm finally really me. Just like the pitch for the product claimed. You guys did a wonderful job on the marketing. And the product is as great as the hype."

"Well, thanks. Uh, that's good to hear." She noticed Jayna's 'self' was dressed in an outfit right out of Emmaline's own closet. She was at a loss of where to go from here. "Any final words, Charlie?"

He raised a brow and shook his head.

"I guess we'll call it a wrap, and if anyone would like to stay and chat, we'll be available for questions. Thanks so much for attending."

The class broke into applause - remarkably enthusiastic for a small venue audience.

Everyone stayed and talked to Charlie, Emmaline or among themselves. Emmaline noticed it was mostly the new *Assimilaire* partakers that talked to her and Charlie. She finally had to point out the time and shoo them all out, so she and Charlie would get a break and some lunch before their second class.

"Whew," she expressed when they were alone. "The newbies were a bit intense. But I noticed the folks that were second-timers weren't too worried about us anymore."

"Yeah, I noticed it too," he agreed. "Makes sense. If they've already become like us, they have no need to get to know us further. Although, they all hung around to talk with each other - presumably because they had plenty in common?"

"I guess you're right. Weird."

"Okay, Batgirl, let's blow Cloneville and hit the streets for lunch."

"I'm with you." Emmaline smiled, appreciative he was of like mind without being freakishly identical to her. She let him lead the way.

= NINETEEN =

The afternoon streets were breezy, but there was no rain. As soon as they cleared the hotel by a block, Emmaline grabbed Charlie's hand. His head swung around in surprise and caught a mischievous look in her eye. She began to run, and he responded by taking great bounds along the sidewalk and pulling her in flying leaps beside him. They slowed down, dropping hands and laughing - breathless and full of fun.

"That was great, Emmaline. I needed that."

"Damn that was good - me too." Her heart thumped an upbeat tune.

"I think the surprise was as welcome as the exercise."

"Yeah, it's been annoying having everything so predictable. I needed to do something crazy that all of those other me's probably wouldn't do. I'm tired of them. I wanted to stretch my wings."

"Well, thanks for taking me on the flight."

Emmaline's heart leaped and beat even faster as his eyes flashed at her.

"This place look alright?" he suggested.

"As long as it's not greasy eggs, I'm in," she agreed.

They enjoyed the hot Thai soup, seasoned with lemon grass, ginger and the sweetness of well-established friendship. They cracked their favorite in-jokes and let the matter of *Assimilaire* disperse in a cloud of laughter.

=

Their lunch get-away ended much too soon, and they were back in the claustrophobic-feeling classroom. Greta and Beatrice came in first. Emmaline noticed their clothing was artistic but not something she had at home. She made a mental note to ask Charlie if he thought the ones who talked to them developed differently than the ones who just saw them. She was distracted trying to remember if Jayna and Steve had the same kind of characteristics, when Greta asked her a question.

"Emmaline? Do you still think we're influenced by your personality?"

"Actually, I'm not sure. I don't know what to think about *Assimilaire's* impact at the conference. You don't look like my clone today. What do you think about it now?"

"After you pointed it out last night, I became self-conscious about my new freedom. I am focused on the things that changed. I'm an introspective person, so I know my processes well. It's strange, but I'm thinking differently.

"Yes, I remember you said you were seeing in a much more artistic manner."

"No, I don't mean I see things differently, or even that I reach different conclusions - though that may be true as well. What I mean is, my thinking process is different. I'm...not myself."

"I know what she means," Bea broke in. "We were talking about it over lunch, and we're both feeling...unusual. I wish I could define it better for you. We came to your class early to see if you could help us understand. Did you know this would happen?"

"No!" Emmaline assured her, "I don't know what to tell you, but I do know this wasn't even remotely anticipated. When we reported back to corporate, they were as surprised as we were."

"So the test subjects did not report a merge with someone else's personality?" Greta asked.

"Well, certainly not in so many words, and not in any way that made it into the summaries of the study data." Emmaline waved her hand at Charlie to call him into their conversation. "You remember Greta and Bea from the Gemini Room?"

He nodded politely.

"They don't feel quite themselves today," she told him.

His hand flipped across his cowlick without his notice.

"Uh, that's right," Greta confirmed, "I feel my thought patterns are different. It's hard to explain."

"Do you mean you follow unfamiliar pathways to draw your conclusions?" Charlie defined.

"Something like that...Yes, that's the idea."

Bea added, "my thoughts are more active. Louder, perhaps. Usually my mind is somewhat quiet, and now I'm constantly evaluating and responding."

"And mine is always this active, but it's more...boisterous. I feel as though my conclusions must be shared. And for each point I consider, there's a starburst of off-shoot ideas. It's somewhat overwhelming." Greta's brow pulled in as she went silent.

"Overwhelming?" Emmaline gave a laugh-snort, "I can't imagine anything else." Then she dropped silent too, as they all felt the weight of her observation.

"Maybe we really are becoming you," Bea said - her features grave.

"First of all, that would be impossible to achieve with the slight chemical change caused by a dose of medication," Charlie said. "And second, there's a lot more to Emmaline than an overactive imagination." He lifted a brow and smirked as if expecting them to share the joke. He was the only one laughing.

"And why would I see more differentiation in your style today instead of less if you were mimicking me more today?" Emmaline tried.

"Actually, I think that would support being more like you," Charlie admitted - serious now. "While we were able to see enough of a pattern to define a style for you, it still has variety at its base.

Plus, if - as they are feeling - this change is at the root level of thought patterns and personality traits, the surface expressions should be varied. Only surface mimicry would produce look-alikes."

"Is it really bad?" Emmaline's eyes grew round with anxiety as she faced the women.

"No," Greta assured her, "it's not all that strange, and it's certainly not terrible. It's just foreign."

"Had you not brought it up to us last night, I'm not sure I would have noticed. I'm in line with the self that I know, just getting there by an unusual path, and I do seem to have more ideas to choose from. It's not at all unpleasant, though Emmaline. Don't worry. If it is you, then you're a fun person to be." Bea flashed a broad smile and her red curls shook with a reassuring nod.

Emmaline leaned back on one hip and let out a deep laugh. "Thank God for that! If we're influencing people, I hope we can at least show them a good time, eh Charlie?"

He tipped his head and shrugged with his palms tipped back wide. Then he flashed his crooked grin. "Nothing but fun - that's Charlie and Emmaline."

They were caught by surprise when a middle-aged man chimed in. "I'll say. I've never had such a good time at a conference as I've had in the last twenty-four hours. Whatever you all packed into that little *Assimilaire* pill - I'm here for more."

The four exchanged hurried glances and stepped back to include him and the others that had come into the room.

"Good afternoon," Emmaline greeted. "Uh, as a matter of fact, we have more free samples for you today if you'd like, and after everyone in the class gets some, you're welcome to take more with you to use or distribute as you wish."

"Sounds great! I'm Sam Boone." He put out his hand to her.

"Nice to meet you, Sam. And this is Charlie." She passed him off hoping to get one more private word with Bea and Greta.

"Uh, hello," Charlie took the cue.

Emmaline grabbed Bea's elbow as she was retreating to a desk. "Greta," she whispered and curled her finger in summons. "Are you two planning to take another dose today?" she kept the volume conspiratorial.

"Should we?" Bea looked to them both for direction.

"It's up to you, but either way, can you let me know how you're doing later? I'm here at the Milieu in room 4023, fourth floor," Emmaline told them.

"Sure," Greta agreed as Bea nodded beside her. "Room Over-the-Hill Conspiracy. I can remember that."

Emmaline's mouth dropped for a second as she recognized her own memorization method. "Great," she said, and then returned to her task of teaching another class of clones, newbies, and mental reflections of herself and Charlie.

While the class visited the water pitchers and samples, she whispered to Charlie that Bea and Greta had agreed to report in later. She forgot to take note of who took the medication, so she was uncertain what her new-found friends - or minions as Charlie called them - had decided to do.

As the class unfolded, it occurred to Emmaline how uncanny the resemblance was to the earlier session. She was spooked by the almost identical answers to her Socratic questions. She preferred that presentation method to outline teaching because of the variety it allowed. Using leading questions to convey information brought up points in an order natural to each group and allowed their answers to suggest new ideas. She could build on them or even learn things herself. But this was the same lesson, in the same order. What should have been the unique dynamic of each group was repeated almost exactly. They were thinking the same as each other. She couldn't wait to discuss it with Charlie.

Once again, they wrapped up early, and she invited the class to stay and chat. Again, everyone stayed, but this time with one exception. An odd fellow that Emmaline would call 'a potato person' left the room as soon as she concluded the formal session. It was odd to call him odd, since the definition of her potato person centered on being profoundly plain and common. The kind of character one would choose to represent a Midwestern farmer's political district. Full of every characteristic that cried out Basic American. But in a room full of Emmaline and Charlie-leaning personalities, he was as strange as a punk-rocker at a women's tea room. To Emmaline, his leaving was the most disturbing thing that happened yet.

She did her best to work through her enamored fans' questions without losing her cool. Charlie chatted with his minions with no less fervor than he had at the Gemini Room the night before. His glee helped Emmaline stay focused when she was tempted to clear the room early to get down to the real questions with Charlie. What difference could a few more minutes make?

At last she saw the clock click over to five-thirty, and she called everyone to attention long enough to send them on their way. Just as the first ones were about to reach the door, Max, one of their capable bouncers from the green room entered, effectively blocking the exit.

"Uh, excuse me," Max spoke. Every eye was riveted to his massive form. "I have an announcement. There's been a bomb threat. It's in effect throughout the Midtown district of Chicago. The mayor and law enforcement community ask that everyone stay in their buildings. A curfew has been put on the streets until further notice. You can move around the hotel freely, but no one will be allowed to leave until the curfew is lifted. Emergency and disaster personnel will be coming through and will be on call as long as necessary to help us and the citizens of Chicago. If you don't have reservations at this hotel for tonight, please go to the front desk to check in so they can work on potential accommodations in case the curfew stays in place overnight. Please remain calm and enjoy your stay at the Milieu."

He withdrew from the doorway, leaving it a hostile hole leading to the unknown beyond. The class attendees filtered out in reluctant waves, predicting and discussing the possible fates of their near future.

= TWENTY =

Charlie hovered over Emmaline as she packed up her laptop and left the classroom. When they got out into the hallway, she couldn't stand it anymore.

"What's up, Charlie? You're clinging to me like double-knit on pantyhose."

"Well, I didn't want you to walk back by yourself. Did you want me to leave?"

"Well, no." She was confused by his behavior. "I mean, I assumed we would eat dinner together, but you're um…" She decided to drop it.

"So I guess we'll stop by your room so you can drop off the laptop and stuff and then go down to the Palm Court?"

"Sure." He was so tight on her that she felt strange about him coming to her room. She couldn't understand why she felt so sweated. They had spent almost the whole conference together, and she hadn't felt claustrophobic before. Maybe it was just the curfew - knowing she couldn't get away from him, or anyone else for that matter. She began to wonder how many of the Emmaline-influenced Assimilairies were trapped here with them.

"You're awfully quiet, Emmaline. Are you worried about a bomb?"

"Just wish I knew how long it would last. Are you worried?"

"Not exactly, although it's unusual to hold people in their hotels. I've only heard of it when there's widespread bombing during acts of war. Like in Bagdad or on the Gaza strip."

"Wouldn't they keep us here if there was a threat at a nearby building?"

"Maybe, but he said the curfew was in effect throughout the whole district, and according to the tourist map we got at check-in, that covers most of downtown proper. There's something bigger going on here."

"Why would they think we'd be safer in the hotels?"

"They might have a tip, or an understanding of the party that put in the threat, that makes them believe a different target would be hit. Plus, they probably need to keep people off the street. They might not actually know we're safe here. But we're contained and they know where to find us."

"That's comforting."

"Sorry."

All of the sudden, Emmaline was glad to have Charlie near - not that he could stop a bomb, but he was a comfort nonetheless. "Do you think it's terrorists?"

"I think it's best not to speculate too much."

"You started it," she said playfully. "We may as well not stress over what we can't control, though." She was glad to change the subject. "The Top office will be in heaven when they hear the Petri dish is bursting with specimen and captive for our further observation."

He laughed.

They dropped off the lappie without incident and headed down for some grub. The lobby was a shuffling mass of bodies. The long lines at the check-in desk were making it hard for the rest of the crowd to maneuver, and when they made it across they were confronted by yet another line. It took them ten minutes to get their name on the one hour wait list for the Palm Court.

"Now what?" Emmaline sighed.

"Maybe we should go see if any of our Emmaline and Charlie friends need a room."

"Yeah right," she giggled.

"No, I'm serious. I mean some of the ones we've gotten to know. Maybe they were staying at a different hotel. We could at least offer."

"Ooo, yeah. Then we could really examine them. Great thinking, Igor."

He smiled sideways. "I really am serious, Emmaline."

"Yeah, okay. We've got an hour to kill, why not. Let's find some roomies."

He shook his head. "Ease up, girl."

Emmaline realized she was being a bit crazy. Charlie's gesture made perfect sense. She tried to get herself together. She was feeling crowded in again. But she knew it was irrational.

"Hey, there are Bea and Greta in the queue. I'll go ask them," Emmaline spouted as she began pushing back through the hubbub.

Charlie shuffled over and scooped up Fred as he was just getting to the desk. They met the girls near the fountain. "You remember, Fred?" Charlie eased.

"Yes, and this is Bea and Greta," Emmaline mirrored.

"I'm so glad to be assured a room," Bea bubbled.

"Yes, thanks Emmaline," Greta agreed. "I didn't realize how on edge I was until you pulled me from the precipice. I don't mind changing plans, but I like to know where I'll rest my head."

Fred gave a crimped smile and slight nod to Charlie.

"I wonder how long it'll be to up our table to a five-top?" Emmaline wondered out loud. She bee-lined for the Palm Court's maître d'hôtel.

As the others arrived to the inner courtyard seating area, she bustled back to them. "He said it will be about forty-five more minutes. We didn't even lose any time. Oh, I didn't mean that the way it sounded, I'm just hungry. I'm glad you're joining us. It'll be fun."

Greta smiled, but Bea was distracted.

"So where were you guys staying before?" Emmaline tried again.

"I was at the Commodore," Fred volunteered.

"We were both at the Embassy," Greta replied. "But we had separate rooms."

"It would be nice if we could at least get our things." Beatrice said, revealing part of why she looked pensive.

"Yeah," Emmaline sympathized. "I would find it hard to be without my own nest."

"Don't worry, Bea. We might be back to our own rooms later tonight. No way to tell." Greta leaned back in her chair. "May as well not worry over what we can't control."

Charlie and Emmaline exchanged a quick glance as they recognized the familiar philosophy.

"True." Bea brightened.

"The Commodore wasn't that great anyway," Fred enthused. "I think it would be fun to spend the night here. I had such a good time talking to you last night, Charlie. And you really got me thinking about how *Assimilaire* might be affecting me. Well, affecting us, actually. Now that so many of us are stuck in the same hotel, we'll probably get a chance to observe what's happening with us and some of the others."

"Yeah," Charlie agreed. "It should be interesting." He gave Emmaline a surreptitious wink.

She almost gave him away with the glowing grin she returned. She covered her mouth with her fist and feigned coughing to muffle her laughter.

They changed the conversation to the safe and mundane, learning that Bea was married and Greta was divorced with two teenaged girls. Fred was still single, but had recently popped the question to his girlfriend of six years. He was getting cold feet now that she had accepted.

"Maybe it's the Charlie gene that's making you uncomfortable," Emmaline suggested as their table was called. "He's quite a loner you know."

"What do you know Emmaline? You're not with me twenty-four seven. Maybe I have a secret girlfriend."

"Knowing you, you probably do," she teased as they sat down. "Charlie's a bit of a mystery man sometimes."

"Well, I've always been an open book," Fred said. "Maybe that bodes well for my future with Diane. It's probably just worry that things will change. We've gotten along so well for all these years. I was hesitant to propose on the 'if it ain't broke' principle. But one of my friends tipped me that she was feeling restless and insecure."

"Yeah," Emmaline put in. "A gal can only go on for so long before she concludes she's not loved."

"Sounds like the voice of experience," Charlie surmised. "Was there someone I don't know about Emmaline?"

"As a matter of fact, yes," she answered honestly. But she didn't elaborate.

"Appears you have your mysterious side too, Emmaline." Greta excused her from their pressure. "Relationships are complicated. Things were always tough between Carl and I. We didn't make it through. And since they hit their teens, I've been having trouble with my girls too. I get overwhelmed by how erratic they are. I'm always struggling to find where I stand with them. I think my own rigidity may be part of the problem. I hope my new-found creativity and confidence will help me relate to them better."

"If you're referring to your Emmaline-ness, I'm not so sure it will help. I'm not much of a kid person."

"Oh, but you're a Life person. I can see that in everything you do. You have a bright spontaneity that's balanced with a forward-moving steadiness. I feel it in myself now." Greta assured her.

Emmaline shivered inside. "Not to get too heavy, but do you all still feel it? Do you feel changed?"

"Definitely," Greta confirmed right away.

"Yes, I admit I'm not the same as when I left home. But I believe I'm just a more confident version of myself," Bea said.

"Definitely changed," Fred stated.

"Did any or all of you take another dose of *Assimilaire* today?" Charlie asked the question Emmaline had wondered about.

"I did," Fred confirmed. "Why not? I feel great."

"I didn't and Bea did," Greta revealed. We made an agreement to experiment since we could compare results.

"And?" Emmaline pushed, trying to be patient.

"I don't think it's been long enough since we took it again to draw any conclusions," Bea answered. "But I can tell you that so far I'm not detecting any new or deeper attitudes than I had yesterday. It could be prolonging the effect, but I'm pretty sure it's not intensifying it."

"So you mean if you're Emmaline with one dose, you're not Emmaline-ier with two?" Greta played back.

"Exactly," Bea replied.

"And I haven't felt my Emmaline-ness wear off," Greta went on. "As I said, I feel like I can deal with my girls with a new outlook. But I also still feel like me. I just have a different level of confidence."

"But couldn't that perspective have come from just getting away for awhile?" Emmaline proposed. "Sometimes being apart from a situation lets things gel in a new way."

"Yes, I know how things can close in on you, and the same routine can make it look impossible to change. But the transformation I feel isn't just from rest or a change of pace. That can give you energy, but this is different. I have a deeper understanding."

"Is it possible you learned something during the time you were mirroring Emmaline, and the knowledge has stayed with you?" Charlie supplied.

"Makes perfect sense to me. Although, I still feel a stronger sense of confidence than I felt before. Do you think confidence comes from knowledge or personality?"

"I think it's part of confidence to add up your successes." Emmaline suggested.

"You mean, to know what you're doing?" Charlie translated.

"Well yeah, if it's similar, you'll know what to do the next time. But even when you come up against something new, having success in the past helps you believe you'll succeed again. I think feeling that you'll know what to do is a large part of confidence."

"Well, I guess we'll need more study to figure out whether your personality or your experience level has changed, Greta," Bea concluded.

"Absolutely," Emmaline confirmed. "And right now I'm going to study the dessert menu."

The others laughed and joined her in a delicious diversion from brain-picking.

= TWENTY-ONE =

Full and content, they moved out to the crowded mezzanine. Emmaline scouted for seats, but it was Charlie who spotted a group restless and ready to leave. He scored them five seats by the fountain.

"The orchids are phenomenal," Bea remarked.

"Oh, the colors! It's hard to believe a color that purple could be natural," Greta agreed.

"And the intricate patterns of violet on white. I love how the spider web of lines brings the eye to the delicate throat of the blossom," Emmaline admired.

"My favorite thing is the shimmer in the firm petals and the intricate structure of the flowers," Bea said.

"This one reminds me of a dragon." Greta laughed as she mimicked its jaws with her hand.

"Yup, three peas in a pod," Charlie remarked to Fred.

He laughed. "It's uncanny. Although I'd have to agree on the exquisite structure. I've never taken the time to look at them before. And each type's so distinct from the others and yet so completely Orchid. Ya know what I mean?"

"Like I made it up myself," Charlie smirked. He was feeling jovial now that his blood sugar was leveled.

"You must be tired, Emmaline," Bea realized, changing the subject. "This is quite a whirlwind."

"Yeah, Charlie and I were supposed to go home already but were asked to stay after things got so…interesting."

"I think I'm getting my second wind," Charlie said. "I could go for some music. The classical they pipe in here gets really old." He raised an eyebrow and scanned the others to see if any would pick up his pun.

Emmaline looked his way and rolled her eyes. The others remained oblivious.

Charlie took note. Their long familiarity was still beyond the scope of the others to know or feel, no matter how much they seemed to think alike. Even Fred didn't notice his joke. It soothed him, and he realized he had been uneasy - for all that he was enjoying the experiment. It was fun to have others understand him, but when it came down to it, he didn't want them to be exactly like him either. He drew inward.

"We could move into the bar," Greta suggested. "I could go for a g-n-t."

"They'll serve us out here if we let them know we'd like drinks." Emmaline piped up, and Charlie wondered if she was trying to squirm out of the squeeze she'd find in the bar area. "I saw the note on one of the tables yesterday. Although now the notice is missing from this table."

Charlie and Fred both cocked their heads to look under the table. The girls giggled at their synchronized head tipping.

"Maybe they're not going to serve out here tonight since everything's so crowded," Fred remarked.

"I'll go see," Bea and Emmaline said in unison. They giggled again.

"I think it would be better for one of us to weave through the crowd," Bea said. "I'd like to go, if it's all the same to you. It's fun to feel so bold. Usually I'd want someone to go with me." She wandered off toward the Gemini Room.

"Interesting," Emmaline observed. "I can't even remember the last time I expected someone to go with me. How 'bout you, Greta? Are you the one who goes to ask or the one who waits to find out?"

"I never thought about it like that," she admitted. "I guess I am second to volunteer. If no one steps up, then I take the responsibility. But I wait to see."

"As you did tonight?" Emmaline noticed.

"Yes, I guess so," Greta pursed her lips, lost in thought.

"Okay, ladies," Fred said, "can we quit analyzing ourselves and talk about the bigger picture?"

"What do you mean?" Greta asked.

"You're talking about your minor differences, but all evening when you were presented with the same circumstances you've responded in the same way. We're trapped together now in an environment of potential crises. What happens if the shit really hits the fan and all of you freak out in the same manner?" he teased.

"Who says we'll freak out?" Emmaline and Greta said in one outraged voice. They looked at each other in alarm.

They all burst out laughing at the irony.

Emmaline was the first to become serious. "Actually Fred, you have an interesting point. What if there really is an attack or explosion and so many of us are the same. There will be an artificial similarity of responses. It might limit our chances of survival."

"Or expand it," Fred reasoned. "If everyone responds calmly and capably, the outcome should be good."

"Hmm." Emmaline's brow furrowed.

"What's the matter, Emmaline? Don't trust yourself?" Charlie jeered.

"Yes, they'll serve us out here," Bea interrupted with her report. "But they've asked that we bring in the order, and then they'll deliver the drinks. May I take your order?" She cocked her hip to one side flirtatiously.

Emmaline laughed her hearty laugh. "I think you know mine."

"Tanq and Tonic?"

"Right-o."

"And Greta the same?"

"No, I think I'll have a Sprite. My stomach's a bit finicky at the moment."

"No shit?" Emmaline bubbled. "That's what I drink when my tummy hurts."

Greta didn't laugh with her.

"Chai tea," Charlie and Fred said together. Their heads pivoted toward each other.

"You saw me order that the other night," Charlie accused.

"I did not; I just had a taste for it," Fred insisted.

"Okay," Charlie conceded. "Two chai teas. Weird." His mouth turned sideways in a disgruntled grimace.

"My treat!" Bea waved her credit card as she buzzed away to talk to the bartender.

"As a matter of fact, Charlie," Emmaline continued as though they had not been distracted, "I don't trust myself in an emergency. Although I'm linear and can follow my mental outline through the most stressful presentation, when I'm thrown into a physically threatening or surprising situation, my first reaction is to freeze and draw a blank."

"Miss Confident and Capable?!" Charlie registered genuine surprise.

"Well, I don't go around dwelling on it or broadcasting it," she scowled at his abrupt jab.

"I'm sorry, Emmaline," he stopped. "I didn't mean to poke at you. I just never noticed that about you."

"I usually control situations as much as possible to avoid shocking moments, or I make sure to observe when the heat rises and get out of the kitchen before it bursts into flame."

"Oooo, you're good," Greta complimented her.

"Ah yes, part of the 'be prepared' thing, no doubt," Charlie put together.

"Yes, actually," she admitted.

"Well, avoiding trouble is a great survival strategy - one of the best," Fred handed her.

"But it's not the best for a crisis that corners you and blows up in your face." She looked down.

"Do you have a first aid kit in your bags?" Fred asked.

"Neosporin and Band-Aids."

"And what else?" Greta encouraged.

"My silk skirt could be torn in strips for tourniquets, and my cotton scarves could be bandages."

"There, see," Greta continued, "what you lack in first response you make up for in resourceful thinking and ample supplies."

"I don't doubt I can be helpful, but someone has to respond at the first shock and order people like me into action. If everyone were me, we'd be in a world of hurt."

"For a moment." Greta tried, "so how 'bout you Charlie? How do you react to things?"

"Hopeless denial until truth slaps me into action. Once there's an incident, my brain mobilizes to defuse the situation. I like things peaceful. Everything that disturbs that calm must be eliminated. If I can't avoid it, I will remove it."

"Sounds excellent!" Fred nodded, hopping on this bandwagon.

"Oh, and I faint at the sight of blood."

"Greaaat." Fred rolled his eyes as the women rolled out rich laughter.

Then their mouths formed a circle of flat lines.

"Damn, what a crazy long wait!" Beatrice threw into their midst. "Why so glum?" She asked after catching their groove for a moment. She dropped into her seat.

"Fred has just taken us for a lovely walk on the Dark Side," Charlie illuminated.

She looked at them quizzically.

"I guess I was a little too serious," Fred admitted. "I just brought up what might happen if the scare turned into something and all of us reacted like Charlie and Emmaline."

"Well, it was very un-Charlie-like to run into it so headlong," Charlie said.

"Not really," Emmaline put in. "You often poke at things you're worried about in order to check them out in case they come to be. You don't yank answers out of people like I do, but when something's on your mind, you continue to bring up the subject until you've thought it through - no matter how far flung your thoughts are between questions."

"So you're saying I'm a focused evader?"

"Something like that. You don't truly avoid things. You just give them lots of space while you work them out."

"So I'm a space evader?" His crooked smile led the group in a round of laughter.

"Well, we know one thing," Beatrice giggled, "if the world goes up in flame, Charlie will keep us smiling."

They eased away from the looming bomb threat as they accepted their drinks from the frazzled but still cheery bar maid. Apparently she could smile in a crisis too.

= TWENTY-TWO =

Despite the fru-fru music, the group of five clung to their seats by the fountain. Greta's trip to the Gemini Room suggested it would be more aptly named Aquarius - stuffed with sardines. "You do not want to go in there," she advised. "Oh, and they're running low on Tanqueray, I'm afraid."

"That's okay," Emmaline answered. "I'm at my limit anyway. Although it doesn't bode well for tomorrow." She flashed her light eyes.

"Cut her off!" Charlie teased.

"No more chai either," Greta informed him.

"Cut him off!" Bea beat Emmaline to the punch line. They giggled together - and then gasped.

There was a deep, gut-quivering boom and everything went black. The emergency back-up lights popped on along the surrounding corridors and in a few spots around the floor as the mezzanine erupted in murmured confusion.

"Oh my God," Bea expressed. "It really happened."

"It did sound like an explosion," Charlie seconded. "Or more, it felt like one."

"I wonder how far away it was?" Fred expressed their mutual question.

137

Emmaline looked bewildered. "It was huge."

"Or very nearby," Bea added.

Greta summed up: "Oh my God."

"Attention, everyone. May I have your attention please?" A man yelled down from the dim balcony one floor above the open square.

> The Milieu Midtown has received word that there has been an explosion at the Chicago City Hall about five blocks from the hotel. Please remain calm. There is no immediate threat to The Milieu nor its guests. The building was closed for the night, so it's expected few people will be affected by the blast. There will be emergency crew on the scene and on the surrounding blocks fighting fire and searching for anyone who may have been hurt in the incident. We need you to continue to respect the curfew. And we would also ask, because of the loss of primary power, that you would retire to your rooms for the night as soon as possible. It will be dark in your rooms but safer there. For now you will not be able to order room service, and please keep phone calls through our system to a minimum. Thank...

A group scream interrupted his sign-off. The walls and floor shook with the vibration of another blast - closer this time. The mezzanine was disturbingly dim.

The girls clung to each other - dumbstruck.

Charlie and Fred both stood in a single motion with the receding aftershock. They turned their heads in calm focus like trainable security cams - observing. A bit more light came on in the center of hallway ceilings and in key spots around the mezzanine suggesting the hotel generator might be kicking in, but the feeble glow brought little illumination.

"Uh, Ladies and Gentlemen," the speaker continued from the balcony. "I urge you to move with orderly haste toward your rooms. You will need to use the stairs. We apologize for the inconvenience. Thank you for staying at The Milieu. We will send word to your rooms as soon as we have further information to keep you apprised of the situation."

Everyone stood that wasn't already standing, and the mezzanine broke into pandemonium. So much for orderly. It seemed all the people who needed the south side were on the north and vice-versa. In the low light it was a struggle for friends that were apart to find each other. And although they were told they'd be notified of developments back at their rooms, there were plenty of busybodies who prattled at adrenaline-induced hyper-speed about every possibility of what occurred and how it would affect them next. It was deafening.

Emmaline and the other gals in their group began to move into the fray, with Emmaline leading toward their room.

"Wait!" Charlie called to them. "It will be better to wait until it clears out some."

She stopped and turned back as if in a trance. The other two followed her without question.

"Since so many others don't understand orderly, let's do what we can by taking a place further back in the line. There's no hurry," Fred pointed out.

"But why do they need us to go right to our rooms then?" Bea raised her voice to carry over the noise.

"Probably to avoid hubbubs like the one we're in. Plus, if we're in our registered places, it's easier to find us," Charlie shouted.

"You mean if something happens to us?" Greta looked alarmed.

"There's no reason to jump to the worst conclusion, but yes, partly. Also to make sure that everyone receives communication on what's going on and how they need to respond. If people are wandering about, it's hard to know who has been updated and who hasn't," Charlie assured her.

"Yeah, don't worry, Greta. There's nothing we can do but follow instructions and then wait and see," Emmaline added.

"But how do we know they won't hit this building next?" Greta voiced the fear at the root of the mayhem.

"We don't," Emmaline admitted, "but it's no good to run amok or cringe in the corner."

"Besides," Charlie reasoned, "that last one was really close. If they chose a target that close that wasn't us, they probably wouldn't pick us too, or they would've done it at the same time."

Their part of the room had emptied to a manageable melee. "Shall we go," Charlie suggested.

"Sure," Fred agreed. "Ladies?" He held out his hand, deferring to them to lead the way through the semi-dark room.

Emmaline started to walk but checked behind her. Charlie read her discomfort and joined her at the front of the group. "Are you okay?" he asked quietly.

"I think so. I'm just tired."

"Well, this was a hell of a stunt to get us to go to bed early. You could've just asked." He brushed his cowlick as he grinned at her. He saw her relax into her pace as they started up the stairs, but wondered what was on her mind.

=

The crowded stairway suggested a polite hush as they all worked their way to the upper floors. The crowd thinned as they neared their destination, and the halls held an eerie mood in the half-darkness.

"Do you guys want to hang out with us?" Greta invited. "Oh, if it's okay with you, Emmaline. I forgot it's your room."

"Wouldn't that be breaking the rules?" Emmaline asked. "We're supposed to be in our registered rooms."

"I think as long as we're associated it's fine," Charlie confirmed.

"Are you really that worried, Emmaline?" Fred asked.

"Uh, no, I mean…it would be great to have you guys along for…"

The end of her sentence was obliterated by a deafening blast. Their blank ears rang in the almost dark hallway. The secondary overheads were out again. Only the emergency corner lights remained.

"Nobody move," Charlie instructed.

"Oh!" one of the women gasped.

"So much for logic," he continued. "Apparently there's been a blast close enough to knock out the hotel's generator."

"Does that mean they've hit the hotel?" Emmaline's voice shook.

"It's hard to know. Let's take first things first and find our rooms. We…"

"But what if it's on fire?!" Greta worried.

"Try to be calm. It's still best for us to find our rooms. We'll be able to see out the windows. Do any of you have a flashlight in your purse, or a lighter or something?" Charlie directed.

"Oh, of course," Emmaline was strengthened. There was a rustling as she rooted for her prize. "My key light!" A bright LED beam testified to her words.

"Homage to Miss Prepared!" Fred cheered, and the women chortled a chorus of nervous laughter.

"Yes," Charlie agreed. "Let's shine it on the nearest door number and get our bearings. Then we'll walk without the extra light to save the life of it. Just in case."

They found they had only six rooms to go. They shuffled along quickly in the nearly dark hall, perhaps anxious to get to the light of a window. Emmaline shined the LED and checked the room number again when she thought they were there. She was one door short. As she moved along to the next one, she got her key card at the ready. Her breath came in quick puffs as her pulse rose in anticipation of getting out of the hall and seeing what was going on in the rest of the world.

She pushed the button on her key light just short of the door. She clicked it open, and they all followed the blue-white beam into the room. The curtain was open from Emmaline's earlier admiration of the view, but the expected flood of clarity from the halo of city lights was disappointingly absent. Instead the walls were bathed in red alert with flashing white and blue accents. They were drawn to the hollow light of the window to see what lay below.

They looked out over a darkened section of the city. The malevolent rosy glow of the night wavered in intensity and their eyes were stabbed by reflections of flashing emergency lights in cracked windows down the block across the street. The sources were hidden. The radiance illuminated mounds of debris scattered at the end of the block to their left. It thinned gradually below them and continued to peter out in the two visible blocks to the right. The smashed façades of the buildings on the other side of the street were the immediate view, through a rain of still-falling lighter particles, and a stream of emergency workers were coming from the area with the flashing lights. The workers disappeared - presumably through a doorway - also to their right below.

"No fire in the hotel judging by the reflections," Fred decided.

"At least not visible to this side," Charlie agreed. "And I think they would've raised the alarm by now if they were working toward evacuation. We should stay put. That stream of EMT's isn't arriving for nothing. There must be a lot more injuries than they anticipated."

Emmaline sank down on her bed and felt more trapped than ever. She wished it was light enough to cross-stitch her excess energy away.

= TWENTY-THREE =

They had just begun to speculate on what had occurred when there was a knock at the door. Emmaline was first over to open it. A warm radiance met her, emanating from a cart full of candles in crystal holders gathered from the bar and restaurants. Only about eight were lit, but they cheered Emmaline like a bonfire on a chilly beach. A young woman lit a new one to hand to her and then smiled in the glow.

"I have a report for you also," the middle aged man with her began.

"Can you wait just one moment," Emmaline asked, "I'd like the others to hear it too."

They had assembled behind her already. Curious and hungry for the diversion, she and Charlie stepped into the hallway so the others could see and hear better.

"The explosions were caused by detonated bombs which were threatened earlier in the day at several sites in nearby civic buildings. The targets that were described by the perpetrators or suspected by investigators have all been hit, and they don't expect the situation to escalate further. The streets surrounding The Milieu are currently blocked with debris, and it's unsafe to leave the building. We won't be receiving any supplies, but some additional light in the halls and mezzanine is expected to be restored within the hour. It was just generator connections that were affected in the shock. We are unable to tell you when you'll be able to leave the hotel, but we will update you as information becomes available."

"Can we leave our rooms?" Emmaline inserted when the man stopped to take a breath.

"I was just getting to that," he said without scolding. "We realize that guests may become restless or need something to eat. The mezzanine area will be open as soon as the generator restores some light. To maintain safety, we'll schedule access to the mezzanine for guests from two floors at a time in one hour increments. We will ring your room phone once when the generator is up and running. Your floor will be welcome from midnight to one, then five o'clock to six, ten o'clock to eleven, et cetera, with five hour intervals as the starting points. We won't have hot food, but should have a selection of cold food and drinks available to sustain everyone." He stopped.

Charlie spoke next, "Thanks for the information. And the light source." He gave them his crooked smile. "Do you have any idea what the origin or purpose of the bombings was?"

"No sir, we have no specifics at this time. The emergency communications are focusing on the basics of safe conduct and the expected schedule to be released from the building."

"Thanks again," he conceded.

"Was anyone hurt?" Emmaline was concerned.

"Yes, there were some injuries. An area of the hotel near the blast zone has been set up for triage. Emergency workers are continuing to arrive to the space."

"Is it serious?" she pressed.

"I'm not sure. We've been asked to stay out of the area."

The young woman leaned into the cart and began moving along the hallway.

The group went back into room 4023, and Emmaline shut the door without feeling shut in this time. She carried the small flickering light like a beacon of hope into the now cozy-feeling space. She found her purse and pulled out her cell phone - 11:30 p.m. Time had really flown. She was surprised, but expected the next half hour to feel like an eternity.

"Anybody for cards?" Greta offered.

"You have cards in your purse?" Fred lifted a brow at her.

"I bought them earlier today in the gift shop. I thought they might come in handy if we got bored between classes."

"Good call," he teased. He lifted the dark lamp from the night stand to the floor and slid the small table out between the two beds where Emmaline centered the candle on it.

Charlie moved a chair over to the gap at the end of the beds and straddled it, as the others bounced into their seats - two to a bed.

"Rummy?" Bea suggested.

"Remind me of the rules," Emmaline said. "I love to play, but I always mix it up with Gin. That's my game, but it only works for two. I hope my 'gin-tuition' rolls over to rummy. I'll beat the pants off you guys." She laughed.

"Strip Rummy?" Charlie jabbed. "Is that possible?"

"One can strip to anything if they try hard enough," Greta quipped.

"I think we should leave our clothes on guys," Emmaline put in. "It's already starting to get cold in here with the power out."

"It'll be back on before we know it." Charlie's eyes twinkled in the candle's flicker.

"Clothes on." Emmaline demanded with a smirk.

"Okay, okay," Fred agreed. "So how do we play?"

Bea ran them through the rules, and soon they were competing and taunting and laughing like old friends. They lost track of the time.

"Hey!" Emmaline exclaimed when she checked her phone between rounds. "It's quarter after twelve. We're missing our time downstairs."

"Uh, the generator power's not on, remember?" Charlie pointed out. "They said we could begin going down after…"

The room phone rang once as he spoke.

"Very funny, Emmaline. You made that happen just to be right, didn't you?"

"Damn tootin'!" she owned.

They all laughed merrily and got up from the game, setting their cards upside-down at their places so they could continue the round when they returned.

Emmaline checked her purse for matches, and after finding a book with five left, she blew out the candle. "Let's go!" She was excited to get out and about.

=

Even with the reduced numbers allowed, the mezzanine was buzzing. It was like a city released after being snowbound. The five managed to get their same spot by the fountain. The reduced light seemed bright after the comparative darkness of their room.

"That's kind of odd we got the same table," Bea remarked as they sat.

"Yeah, what are the chances?" Greta agreed.

Emmaline noticed the laughing groups assembled around them. "It's kind of strange how cheery everyone is."

"What do you want us to do," Charlie answered, "mope?" He looked pensive.

"Well, no," she admitted, "but that was a pretty serious mess out there. I'm concerned about the injuries. And we heard at least three blasts. There could have been more."

"Yes, we're aware of that Speaker of Gloom. But we've been asked to stay put and stay out of it. What's the point of dwelling on the negative?" Fred said. He leaned back in his chair stretching his legs out in full lounging mode.

"There's nothing wrong with staying in touch with reality." Greta defended Emmaline.

"It's part of being prepared," Bea agreed.

"Plus, I feel bad just sitting here if there are people in need," Emmaline confessed.

The waitress came to check on what they wanted. She smiled like it was any other day.

Emmaline was interested to see that all three girls ordered Sprite. Charlie and Fred ordered water and a basket of bread.

"I'm prepared all the time," Charlie continued after the waitress was gone. "I'm the one who pops into action when hell breaks loose. Just because I seem laid back doesn't mean I'm not 'in touch with reality'. Avoiding the subject just keeps constant tension from pushing me over the edge. It keeps my energy up for when I can help."

"Makes sense," Emmaline nodded.

"Excuse me," a woman approached their table with a guy at her elbow.

They all came to attention.

"Oh, don't worry," she said when she saw their serious faces, "I just wanted to see if you'd mind if we join you. We were in your class earlier, and we thought it would be fun to chat, if that's okay?"

"Oh…sure," Charlie allowed.

"I'm Stacey and this is Ben," she introduced as they pulled up chairs.

Emmaline scanned them for pseudo-Charlie and semi-Emmaline characteristics. Then she remembered they might not have access to their suitcases let alone shops. They couldn't express their newly found tastes - if they had them. "Hi there," she greeted. "Were you guys staying at The Milieu or are you fugitives of fortune?"

They smiled. "I was staying at the Commodore, but Ben here was kind enough to let me hang out at his room. We met during your class and kind of bonded in the crisis."

"Nice," Emmaline grinned.

"I just thought it would be fun to hang out with a larger group for a while," she continued.

Everyone shifted as they adapted to the change. Ben checked his cell. "I'm waiting for a call back from my daughter," he explained. "She left a message on my voicemail while I was in the chaos getting out of the mezzanine earlier. I didn't hear the ringtone. She's in government work and had heard there was some kind of threat in downtown Chicago. She told me not to call, but that she'd call back later to check in. I don't want to miss her and leave her worried."

"Oh," Greta gasped, "do you think this has been covered on the news? I better call my daughters and let them know I'm okay. I can't believe I didn't think about it. I was in my own little world."

"Don't feel bad, Greta," Emmaline said. "We had to figure this out before we got worried about everyone else."

"It's just not like me to forget my kids," Greta fretted.

Emmaline ticked off another likeness point. She was in her own world much of the time. And though she was generous and cared for others when she interacted with them, she was almost as much of a loner as Charlie. Other people often fell into the outta-sight-outta-mind category.

Bea sat with her head downcast. "I forgot my husband too. I can't believe I let him down. If he's heard, he'll be beside himself. I must contact him whatever the roaming charge." She opened her purse and pulled out her cell.

Emmaline and Charlie looked at Fred.

"I don't have a cell phone," he confessed.

"I don't have anyone to call," Charlie said. "Well, I guess my sister might worry."

"Your sister will definitely worry, Charlie," Emmaline said.

"But she knows I don't usually call, so she'll be okay with it."

"It'd be nice to ease her mind though," Emmaline pushed him.

"Yeah, alright." He tucked his hand into his inside jacket pocket.

Emmaline sat tight. She felt empty having no one to call - growing restless as everyone chatted on their phones except her and Fred. She excused herself, assuming Fred would think she was seeking the restroom. She actually went toward where she thought the last blast may have come from, using her memory of the front of the hotel to work toward where they had seen the thicker pile of debris. She opened a hallway door and saw a sign on the door at the other end that read, 'Emergency Response Area- No Guest Entrance'. She pushed her way through.

=

The others began to chat with Stacey and Ben as they finished their calls. The two were from Buffalo and told how they had laughed about it when they met. "I come all the way to Chicago and meet the girl next door?" Ben smirked.

Charlie's brow went up. "Hey, where's Emmaline? It's almost time to go back to the room."

"I think she went to the restroom," Fred supplied. "She left while you guys were on the phone."

"Must be one heck of a dumper," Charlie jabbed. "She should be back by now." His smile disappeared.

"Maybe she bumped into someone she knows," Bea suggested.

"Or she decided to act on her concern and go find out who's injured," Charlie said, knowing her only too well.

"Would she do that?" Greta asked.

"Would you?" Charlie asked her back.

Greta thought for a moment. "I must admit I haven't been able to let it go. The whole time we were talking I was trying to think how I might help."

"Me too," Bea confirmed.

"Me too," Stacey's brow wrinkled in surprise.

"Let's go," Charlie groaned to Fred and Ben. "These women are never going to quit."

= TWENTY-FOUR =

The group pushed through the door marked No Guest Admittance and were shocked by the bloody horror that met their eyes. Charlie, Fred and Ben abruptly fainted.

"Great!" Greta turned on her heel and all three girls stooped to revive the guys.

As they started to come around, Bea went to where there were pitchers of water and brought back full cups for them. The guys sat up and drank, averting their eyes from the injured.

"Big help you are," Bea scolded. Her tough glare faded when they looked defeated. "It's okay. Just stay here and let us take care of things for a few minutes," she encouraged them.

Greta and Stacey had already found Emmaline and were helping her, and two other women they recognized from class earlier, move a man with a flayed femur from the floor to a table top on a stretcher. An EMT instructed them. The worker began to clean and close the wound to staunch the bleeding.

The girls continued to aid the medical teams however they were told. And more women - including Jayna Pritchet who they'd met at the Gemini Room - joined them coming in through the door from the mezzanine. Every once in a while a guy or two would come through the door after their women friends and fold to the floor unconscious.

Charlie and his minions stayed at the ready - backs to the injured - to revive those who passed out. It would've been funny if it wasn't so dire.

Each time they cleared the room of wounded, the EMT's took time to clean up and hydrate before another wave arrived. Fred and Ben went several times to ask hotel personnel to refill the water pitchers and supply more cups. They also brought back crackers and fruit.

"Oh!" Emmaline's emotion broke the routine of care that had been flowing forward without a hitch. "Zenia!"

The reporter's bubbling intensity was reduced to a weak desperation. There was a gash in her left shoulder that was bleeding heavily. She was brought in first of the new group for urgent treatment. Emmaline froze.

"You three, help here please," an EMT commanded. "You," she pointed at Emmaline, "take a break for water, then go help your friend and Jackson in the back corner."

The routine began to move ahead again as Emmaline wandered away as instructed. She wiped away tears as she swallowed the water Charlie gave her.

"Are you okay, Em?" He laid his hand on her shoulder.

"Yeah, I saw Zenia. It's different when it's someone you know. But I've gotta help Marta and Jackson." She pulled away and returned to her mission with grim determination.

At long last, the parade of burned and debris-riddled victims came to an end. The EMT's worked with the women to make sure they were cleaned to sanitary and well on their way to hydrated before they would dismiss them. They also gave each one a final piece of fruit to consume.

"You were a Godsend," an EMT told Emmaline as she showed her how to scrub. She was the same one that had redirected her when she froze over Zenia. "Where did all of you gals come from? Are you with a volunteer group or something? We could use more people like you."

"Not exactly," Emmaline replied, her eyebrow going up at the irony of the woman's last remark. "We don't even know each other for the most part."

"It's uncanny how well you work together. So like-minded. You all took instruction well too," she noticed, "even when you recognized your friend you listened and responded instead of giving in to the shock."

"'Works well with others,' yes, I've heard that all my life." Emmaline smiled. Then her brow furrowed. "Will Zenia be alright?"

"Yes, I think so. She had lost a lot of blood, but we were able to begin hydration and she was responding well when they moved her to be held for transport. I wonder why she was caught in the blast? Did she break curfew and leave your group?"

"She wasn't really with us. I just met her once. She's a reporter."

"Oh, enough said. Crazy fools."

Emmaline agreed with a soft grin, and then her face burst into a wide yawn that she demurely covered. "Oh my God, I'm exhausted."

"Well, it is six-thirty in the morning," the EMT said. "You've been up all night."

"Oh!" Emmaline exclaimed. She looked over to see the guys crashed out on chairs over in one corner. The rest of the women were saying good-bye to the new friends they partnered with for the last several hours.

"Wait!" Emmaline called to the group. "I just want to confirm something before you all disperse."

The group moved toward her, many of them wobbly on their feet now that their adrenaline was dropping to more normal levels. They looked curious to hear what she had to say.

"Were all of you in my classes yesterday?" she asked.

There was a nod of assent from every sleepy head. They exchanged glances in alarm.

"Yes, kind of spooky, isn't it?" Emmaline gloried in their expressions. "I'm glad I'm not the only one who thinks it's scary. This is just too much. How many of you think you would've come into a room marked No Admittance and insisted on helping strangers all night before you took *Assimilaire?*"

Less than a quarter of the group of women raised their hands. The rest shifted, looking uncomfortable.

"Do you feel different?"

"Just more confident and interested in what's around me," Jayna observed. "I still feel like me. I am myself, aren't I?" Her blonde bob flipped as she looked back and forth at the others.

"Yes, I think so," Emmaline assured without conviction, "but my friends who have taken the drug said they felt like they had changed. Bea, Greta, how are you feeling now?"

"I feel exhausted," Greta said simply.

"Me too," admitted Beatrice. "And I know I wouldn't have done something like this before, but it doesn't feel strange to me. I still feel like the same Bea that came here - just deeper."

"Okay, ladies. Let's get some rest." Emmaline concluded.

"Are we gonna be okay?" Jayna asked.

"I'm sure after some rest you'll be just fine," Emmaline said.

"No, I mean from the *Assimilaire.* I don't like the idea of being someone I'm not."

"Well, the effects wear off, but judging by what Greta and Bea have reported, you might change a little from some of your experiences during the time you have a different perspective."

"Why did we become like you?" another woman asked.

"I'm not sure," Emmaline admitted. "Perhaps because I was the dominant woman presented when you took it."

"Does that mean if I took some at home I would become my mother?" a young woman asked, her eyes wide.

Emmaline hesitated, her imagination gripped by fear. "We don't really know. In the studies the subjects didn't take *Assimilaire* together in a group, so this characteristic of picking up the thought patterns or personality of someone else wasn't noticed. The subjects reported feeling like they related to the people around them more harmoniously. Of course if they became like-minded to the person or people they were with they would feel more unity with them. But the question of whether they were becoming someone else was never asked, and the observation was never reported. The only reason we've realized this here is because so many took it at once and then were kept together in one place."

"What if someone takes it around a criminal? Will they become evil?"

"Or if they take it around someone who's really prejudiced, will it affect their judgment of others?"

"Or what if people continue taking it around those of us who have become more like you, Emmaline, will all the women eventually become Emmalines?"

The women's intense questions firing at her overwhelmed Emmaline's exhausted psyche. "I don't know. I don't know," she cried out, and to her complete surprise she burst into tears.

The others crowded around to comfort her, but it just upset her all the more. Finally she took a deep breath and called out, "Can I get some air, please?"

They backed off. "Sorry, Emmaline," several of them offered. They retreated to some nearby chairs and leaned against the walls until she calmed down. Bea and Greta stayed near her, and she was glad. She wanted comfort, just not a crowd - especially one that was so bizarre to her.

"I'm sorry," Emmaline said to the group as she caught her breath and got a grip.

"It's okay, we understand," Jayna said.

"I'm sure you do," Emmaline burst into laughter as fully as she had burst into tears. The room roared with hearty guffaws and belly laughs. She took advantage of their camaraderie to instigate a plan. "I understand by your questions, and the fact that you all hung around to ask them when you are so tired, that you're as concerned about the ramifications of this medication being on the market as I am. I don't think we can just sit back and wait to see what happens. You all mobilized for the need of the bombing victims, and I'm hoping I can count on you to help plan the demise - or at least recall for more research - of *Assimilaire*. Today is the last day of the conference. I'm assuming most of you are planning to head home as soon as they let us out of here, but is it possible to meet before we go?"

"My flight's at two-thirty this afternoon," one woman volunteered.

"Mine's at..." another began.

"Wait," Emmaline interrupted. "Does anyone have a flight before two-thirty?" she asked logically.

No one indicated that they did.

"Okay, then. Let's get some rest until about twelve-thirty and then meet by the fountain in the mezzanine. I know it's not much rest, but we haven't got much time. Deal?"

"Deal!" the women spoke in one voice and then erupted into laughter again.

"I'll see if I can get some of the Charlies to help us in our quest to turn this mess around," Emmaline told them as they headed for the doors.

"Speaking of Charlie," she said to Bea and Greta, "let's get the sleepy little boys up and get 'em outta here." She began to do just that.

They gave Charlie and crew time to come out of their dream worlds - it helped that the rumbling laughter of the women had roused them - and then they headed out to their rooms. Emmaline filled Charlie in on her conference with the Emmalines and told him how even the EMT's had noticed how alike they were. "Would you be willing to round up some of the Charlies before the meeting? I'd like you guys in on this. Then you and Fred can meet us beforehand at my room - say noon?"

"Sure, Emmaline. I think I must have been asleep for quite a while, so I'll just stay up." He moved away from her. "Hey, Fred," he called, "will you help me find some more of the Charlie clones?"

Some of the other guys agreed to help, and the guys peeled off from the girls and went back towards the mezzanine.

"Oh, what about the hourly plans for when we're supposed to be downstairs," Emmaline remembered out loud.

"I think under the circumstances we'll just have to break the rules," Greta's face showed discomfort. Emmaline's mirrored it.

Bea turned to them with a similar expression. "Yeah, I think it will be okay. This is important. And it has to do with public safety - just like their rules."

Emmaline drew the key card through the slot and heard the satisfying click of the door release. Greta held Emmaline's LED light to beam the way to the crystal candle. Emmaline fumbled for one of her five matches and lit it. "Damn, good thing I've got a double room!" she said, eyeing the extra pillows. "I'm in the bed on the left, girls. Last one to sleep is a rotten egg."

They were apparently too sleepy to offer a jibe regarding the stupid cliché, and all three dropped into bed like they had worked all night saving lives.

Emmaline blew out the candle. She sat up again after setting her head on the deliciously welcome pillow, and with a rueful frown she squinted into the light to set her cell phone alarm for eleven forty-five.

= TWENTY-FIVE =

Emmaline pulled out of a dream doing her best to identify the meaning of the sound of her own alarm. Her mind just didn't want to acknowledge it as time to wake up. She smacked the phone to snooze and remembered the big meeting.

"Aargh," she groaned loudly, despite the women just awakening in the bed beside her. "Sorry girls, you can sleep for another half hour. Do you want me to reset the alarm?"

"Mhmm," came in unison from the opposite bed.

Emmaline set it for twelve fifteen and left her phone by Greta's head. She was buoyed by the daylight coming into the room, but lit the candle in its crystal decanter to see in the bathroom. She washed up, brushed her teeth and dressed way too quickly. The image in the mirror looked as hellish as she felt. She did what she could to improve it to tolerable, doused the candle, grabbed her purse and wandered out into the hallway.

"If I had any sense, I'd have told Charlie I'd meet him at his room so we wouldn't disturb the others," she mumbled to herself. By the time it came back to her ears, she realized it would've destroyed her back-up plan to have him knock to wake her if she didn't get up. Miss Prepared. She pressed out a grin.

As her knuckles knocked the surface of Charlie's door, it pulled away from her.

157

His face lit up when he saw her. "You're looking charming this morning, Emmaline," he snipped.

"Shut up, Charlie," flung from her lips with practiced ease. "We're not gearing up for a fashion show."

"Aye, aye, Captain." He saluted at mock attention.

"Is Fred joining us?" she peered in behind him.

"He's still out recruiting, Sir."

She laughed despite herself.

As they walked down the enclosed hall, they both halted and blinked when full power brought the lights up to normal levels.

"Ah, that's a good sign," Charlie commented.

A hotel worker agreed as he approached them, "Yes, sir, it is. I'm coming around to tell the guests we should soon be able to leave the hotel. The streets have been marked and cleared enough to pass safely with detours and there are no new threats."

"Excellent!" Charlie responded as they left the man behind.

"Good for Chicago," Emmaline told Charlie, "but now we're going to have to work fast to find the Assimilaries and decide how we can stop the spread of the drug."

"I'm just glad for no more injury and trauma," he insisted.

"Of course, you're right, Charlie. I totally agree." She picked up her pace indicating belief in her own statement as well. "Did you and Fred find out anything else about the bombings? What was it all about?"

"A staff worker in the mezzanine said it was claimed by a local ring that professes to be part of an international terrorist group. They protest the treatment of Muslims by governments in predominantly Christian countries. But the larger organization hasn't taken responsibility or admitted the group was sanctioned by them to do this."

"Well, this should work wonders to bring the trust and unity they're fighting for." Her voice oozed sarcasm.

"The intelligence so far shows no connection outside of Chicago other than the group's ideals. Lucky for us, it's considered an amateur attack. Other than the fact there were several sites hit, the damage was reported as minimal. They're also saying injuries were minor, although I saw more than enough blood last night."

"I saw plenty enough too, but we received the injured from three of the five blasts, and none were critically wounded. I would imagine that's small potatoes from a terrorist attack point of view."

"Yeah, terrorists in their own minds. But it was enough to make us all pretty edgy, that's for sure. I'm just glad it's over."

"Seconds to that!" Emmaline agreed.

They came out to a mezzanine full of life. The hotel staff was responding to the power being on - rearranging the area, collecting some of the things that had been brought out from the restaurants - so they could put their regular service back into place.

"Do you think we should still meet out here?" Emmaline asked. "It seems very exposed with all this traffic and the lights on. I forgot when planning that the natural light would shine down on us from the skylights with noonish intensity too."

"I don't think our plans are really secret. And we don't have anywhere else that will have a big enough space. We're just going to talk over how people are feeling and if we think it's a threat to society, right?"

"Well, that's what you and I need to decide. What are we gonna do?" She turned and walked away from him toward a woman clearing a nearby table. "Excuse me, will we still be able to get food service here?"

"Yes, ma'am. The hot menu may still be limited, and I think we're out of some items but…"

"Okay, we'll take this table when you're done, and I'll go order something from the bar. Thanks." She waved Charlie over to join her.

"I'll go get us something. Any preference?" she asked him.

"No meat," he twitched a grin at her.

"Yeah, yeah. Okay, hold down the fort."

Charlie was talking to Fred when Emmaline returned just a couple minutes later.

"So do you guys have it all worked out?" She raised an eyebrow.

"How could we possibly make a plan without the mighty Emmaline?" Charlie quipped.

"Okay, boys, spill it."

"Well," Charlie paused. "The guys Fred's been meeting with agree they see some changes in themselves, but most of them don't see it as a problem. They're mostly concerned about what will happen when the drug gets out there with a bad model to mirror. Like these wacko guys that did the bombings - suppose they distributed it at some kind of initiate meetings and increased their ranks. Or anyone else with negative or evil ideas and intent. I know most of the guys coming to our meeting today want to talk about that."

"Yeah, the women were raising the same kind of questions. But they were worried about the more subtle effects too, like having too homogenous of a personality type emerge. Last night during the crisis it was obvious that it's important to have various types of people to perform different important tasks. If too many people move to one way of being, and one mode of thinking, we could be caught with our pants down and our keisters flappin' in the breeze." Emmaline said.

"I think that pretty much says it," Fred agreed. "We should just outline these basic points and let those that show up for the meeting weigh in with their experiences and concerns and go from there."

"Wing it. Good plan, my man," Charlie flashed a grin.

"I do think it kind of plans itself. It's not winging it, it's just obvious," Emmaline said. "Ooo and these are obviously our snacks!"

The waitress set down two plates of assorted Mediterranean-themed delights. Dolmas, olives, hummus and pita - it smelled divine. And the second platter had heated pita appies with tapenade and dabs of goat cheese on top. Charlie and Emmaline dived for the warm ones. Fred popped a couple Kalamatas in his mouth and left the rest.

As the food dwindled on the plate, a crowd formed at the surrounding tables, and Fred walked around greeting some of the pseudo-Charlies he had contacted beforehand. Emmaline wiped her lips daintily with her napkin and chatted to some folks from the group, hoping they would excuse her garlic-olive breath. At least it was freshly tainted.

Beatrice and Greta appeared three tables away from Charlie and Emmaline looking about as put together as Emmaline had when she arrived. She stole over and suggested they order something to eat and promised she'd wait to call things to order until they returned. Greta disappeared over toward the Gemini Room. Her return ten minutes later triggered Emmaline to nod to Charlie to get things rolling. The two of them stepped up on the fountain's wide edge using it as a stage visible to all the tables of Assimilairies.

"Good afternoon," Emmaline began with Charlie giving a wave beside her. "Thanks so much for coming today. I understand you're all here because you have concerns about your experience with *Assimilaire* during the last day or two. Charlie and I were originally excited to offer and promote this new product, but with the unexpected popularity it produced after the kick-off meeting, we were overwhelmed with confusion. Eventually that changed to discomfort and then worry. We've become alarmed enough to call this meeting. We'd like you to share your thoughts, and then we'll come up with a course of action if needed." She nodded to Charlie.

"Um, it's been fun to meet so many of you in the last couple days, and I hope you've had as much satisfaction from our conversations as I have. But after last night's crisis and two days to see these things play out, it has ceased to be a romp. We started to contemplate all kinds of problems that could occur if this drug goes into wide circulation." He eyed the audience.

"As Emmaline said, the response after our presentation surprised us. It caught our corporate administrators and the product developers off guard as well. In the product testing, the subjects were never presented with a strong central model, and it was never taken in a group setting. Because the subjects were separated and reported on their experiences from their own perspective, the mirroring of psyches that we've experienced here was never noticed. The subjects always reported identifying with, and feeling in harmony with the others around them, but they never said they became them - or very like them."

Emmaline picked up the thought. "By the time we got to the end of our evening at the Gemini Room the night before last, it was evident to us that those who had taken *Assimilaire* were taking on our characteristics. Takes one to know one, or something like that - we saw it clearly." She shuddered. "And though it was amusing in some ways, it also became extreme enough for us to mention it to our corporate heads. They asked us to remain at the conference and observe what occurred - especially with those who took further doses. We agreed to teach a couple of classes and hand out more samples, after we were assured there would be no long term effects."

"How do they know that?!" a woman with a bright-colored scarf interrupted.

"That was based on the research showing that all residual trace of the drug is out of subjects' systems within seventy-two hours," Charlie answered.

"But what about our minds?" another woman called out.

"Yes, what about your minds and your own identities?" Emmaline continued. "You have gone to the heart of it for sure. Because of the bomb scare, our second class was confined to The Milieu along with many of you that had taken *Assimilaire* earlier. Charlie and I got to know two women and one guy at a couple of our appearances, and we asked them to stay with us. During our confinement, we found out some remarkable things. One was that the drug's effects went deeper than mimicry. These friends felt they were themselves, but they exhibited Charlie's or my characteristics of personality and thought patterns. Another thing was their experience while in these thought modes shaped them differently, and we realized that could change them even after the medication wore off."

"And then we had the bizarre but blatant evidence of similar character when woman after woman came into the area where guests were not allowed and helped apply first aid to the bombing victims like Emmaline did." Charlie broke in. "And several men came to find where the women had gone, and like me, fainted at their first sight of blood. This left us to worry what would happen if communities became too homogenous in character. Would they be unable to deal with crisis if they mirrored the wrong people or had the same limited skill set? And what if the model or group was chosen maliciously. Emmaline and I were imagining what could happen if a gang like the fanatics who took responsibility for the bombings distributed *Assimilaire* in their meetings. It would be even more dangerous than conventional brainwashing. Those that were *Assimilated* would not only mimic information, but their ability to evaluate what they were learning would be compromised by the same thought patterns and personality leanings as the fanatics who brought them in." When Charlie stopped, no one said a word.

Emmaline broke the silence. "After following through on just a few of the ramifications of having this drug available on the market, we decided we want to do something about it. We no longer think the claim of 'harmless' is applicable. We thought no one would understand our concerns more than those of you who have experience with it and who have been affected. Going back to corporate on our own will be useless. The drug has been touted as a break-through success. It's poised to make them millions. Even if we are all interested in stopping its distribution it will be a long shot. But first, we wanted to know - do you agree? Do you want this stopped?"

A young man stood up. "I'm one of the guys who had the unfortunate trauma of fainting in the triage area last night." He gave them a twisted smile. "I'm a trained EMT. Not only did I have no immediate urge to help the wounded, I literally could not do it. I came in to find my friend Amanda, and I was down for the count. Even if this effect wears off, it'll be in the back of my mind and create hesitation. But worse, as you said, I thought about what would happen if this characteristic was widespread. What if the drug was taken in a small community where there was a model like Charlie, and there was no model like Emmaline to balance it out. People could bleed to death while there were ten others passed out unable to aid them. Crazy stuff! And not harmless. Yes. I want it stopped."

"And I don't know about the rest of you, but I like who I am. It's been interesting to see with an artistic sensibility, but that's not the character I'm used to or that I've built my life on. And what if

Emmaline has more sinister characteristics that have yet to manifest themselves?" A middle aged woman spoke out.

"I do leave my shoes all over the house," Emmaline admitted and laughed her deep laugh. Instead of a round of hearty laughs in response, she heard some snickers from the men and saw a light of recognition go on in the faces of several women. She felt totally strange.

"Excuse me, may I have your attention please," came a voice from above the Mezzanine. The man went on as the crowd quieted, "We have received word that the curfew has been lifted. You can come and go from the Milieu as you wish. Thanks again for your co-operation during the crisis. We welcome you to stay at the Milieu now and on future visits to Midtown Chicago," he concluded and was cheered by the relieved crowd of guests.

As the *Assimiliaries* shared the joy, Emmaline became all the more intent on their meeting. "This is great news! But we need to finish getting your comments now before you're on your way. Does anyone have anything else to share?" She focused them.

"I think the threat of criminal use or the multiplication of menacing factions is the most dire issue," a very Charlie-like-down-to-the-haircut guy said.

The group sobered as they listened to him. "We could debate on the pros and cons of widespread conformity of characteristics, but the cons who blow up buildings are trouble without a doubt. To take it to the extreme, what if someone like Hitler were to use this thing to build up supporters. Not only would they follow him, but they would evaluate new situations like him. They would never rebel against his orders, because they would feel the same motivation that was behind those orders. Certainly your corporate big-wigs would have to bow to the fact that's a dangerous long-term effect."

"Well, that's the next issue, isn't it?" put in Charlie. "How do we get them to listen - let alone bow to anything?"

"If all of you will go back to your rooms or use your travel time to write a testimonial of what you have learned about *Assimilaire* this weekend, and send it in for Charlie and I to present as part of our report on the great WWPA Con experiment, it might make a difference. Please raise your hand if you're willing to do this, and we'll come around to get your name and email address. We'll give you an email address to send your testimonial to by Monday. I know that's tomorrow, and you'll be tired, but this could be a matter of life and death. At the very least it's a matter of important social change." To her relief, every semi-Emmaline and pseudo-Charlie wanted to be a part of the report. Her heart beat with excitement. This was a presentation she really wanted to succeed.

= TWENTY-SIX =

Emmaline sat back in her seat and snapped on her belt ready for take-off. She heaved a huge sigh. She and Charlie had barely made it to the gate in time to board. She'd insisted on making sure every partly-Charlie and semi-Emmaline who wanted to help with the petition had the information to contact them with their report. Charlie had even gone up to their rooms and packed her stuff as well as his own, so she could keep talking to their minions. She looked at him sprawled out into the aisle.

Charlie turned under the intensity of her gaze. He dropped his head back and lolled out his tongue to tease her yet again about what a chore it had been to pack her stuff.

She stuck out her tongue at him, and then giggled. It felt great to relax. She wasn't even worried about take-off. Nothing to do till she was home and could begin gathering emails to create the report-slash-persuasive-speech to get corporate to pull the product. The plane roared down the runway and leaped into the sky. She stopped looking forward, swabbing the focus from the lens of her consciousness, and reached for sleep.

=

Charlie spied on Emmaline's peaceful features, relieved that she had shut down at last. The corners of his mouth lifted as he thought of her courage and spark throughout the weekend. The world really could use more Emmalines. He was pulled from his musings by a light tap against his leg. "Oh, excuse me," he said to the flight attendant whose face maintained an earsplitting smile. He reeled in his legs.

After she passed he leaned out to look toward the back of the plane. He spotted the guys from their crew a few rows back, and waved before pulling back into his seat. That was one of the strangest discoveries of the weekend. Calvin, Ronny and Jason had taken *Assimilaire* at the opening rally, and they were full-on pseudo-Charlies when they came out of the woodwork at the final meeting by the fountain. A trio of beer-slinging, rocker dudes tamed to retro-styled semi-geeks who spoke in full sentences - if that didn't convince corporate nothing would. Not that it showed any blatant danger to society. Although someone had to do their jobs. What if all the roadies just wanted to sit at monitors? Charlie smirked at the thought, leaned back and dozed off himself.

=

Emmaline lugged her overstuffed bag up onto her shoulder and gave the cabby a generous tip. She fumbled with the security door anxious to get to her email. A regular steam train of huff-n-puffs, she arrived in the doorway of her apartment and dropped her bag and ditched her shoes. She bee-lined to her computer and hit the button to boot it up while she made a pit stop and got some grape juice for energy. While taking a good slug of juice, she took a moment to view the lights along the bay below. Home. She settled in - at least it was before midnight. Barely.

=

Charlie jimmied the building lock dreading the task ahead. He was as interested as Emmaline in getting *Assimilaire* off the market but was not as zealous as she at taking the task in hand. Nevertheless, he had agreed to screen the emails right when he got home. He would have to forward his favorite emails and his comments to her before going to sleep. He found some relief as he opened an email from Jensen - they had been given permission for late arrival to work. He could sleep in until eight - great.

=

As she was working her way through the fifteen or so emails that had already arrived, she saw pop-ups begin to appear from Charlie. He either read and processed like lightning or he was choosing and responding as he went. She had decided to read them all through before proceeding, but she couldn't keep her curiosity in check and interrupted her flow to check Charlie's latest send.

My experience with Assimilaire *was one of the most pleasant of my life. I found a confidence that I had never had, and all the colors of the world came alive to my eyes. Where I had been withdrawn, I was suddenly bold. Where I had been cerebral, I was outwardly expressive. But I lost myself. I'm a high level mathematician and bioengineer. As my mind reveled in visual creativity and social freedom, I lost focus for the detail of my craft. It's not that I forgot what I know, but I lost touch with it. My framework changed. It was a struggle to recall the intricate connections of things, and I believe my potential for original work may be seriously compromised. I realized this after taking a second dose and then inexplicably spending my night helping bombing victims in triage - as apparently Emmaline would naturally do. I can stop taking* Assimilaire *and hopefully return to my higher intellectual patterns and pursuits, but I don't want to. Because of this frightening desire, I beg you to remove this pharmaceutical from the market. If you don't, we may all lose the ability, or at least desire, to create the products that you depend on for your livelihood and that may save rather than strangely alter lives.*

--Martha Able, San Hernando, CA

Note: What more can I say? –Charlie

"Wow," Emmaline spoke out loud. The first few she had read had not been that deep. No wonder Charlie had sent it right away. It was pay-dirt - no doubt.

She read on and then went back and pulled a well written essay on the potential danger of having it fall into criminal hands, by a guy named Jerry from Duluth. She added her own remarks relating it to the bombers that wreaked havoc on Chicago while they were there. The concept of creating armies of sociopaths and fanatics was the gravest consequence that could come of the drug, and the easiest point to push. Mortal fear. Losing the wonder of high level thinkers was just not as intense to the imagination as gaining the terror of large gangs made up entirely of Charles Mansons. She shivered with horror and lack of sleep. Three in the morning.

While she was trying to decide which one to use next, a new one came in. From Jeanine in Ohio, *What would happen if no one would vote?* Emmaline was intrigued.

I first noticed my personality shift when I returned to my room after the kick-off and turned on the television. I'm news addicted and follow politics avidly. But I'm not a typical victim of CNN-ification, I studied political science and sociology, and I'm interested in the protection of human rights within our legal and political structures. I found an interview with an author discussing his research on the erosion of rights in times of crisis among the poor sectors of society - such as was grossly illustrated in the South during hurricane Katrina. I had been anticipating this book's release. I changed the channel. Without conscious thought, I moved to a nature show with gorgeous shots of the open lands in Patagonia. I felt fulfilled in watching the wistful winds whistling across the wilds. I forgot my passion for the oppressed.

Oh, don't get me wrong, I still care about the plight of the abandoned poor, but I couldn't stand to hear it discussed in a manner I now consider hopeless to affect change. I no longer believe in the system. My focus has become inner and localized. As I watched the chilly mountain tops teeming with remote life, I felt the lonely angst of the downtrodden. I believe I would've given my dinner to a homeless man right then, but I would not have supported a political system to help him. I realized in this frame of mind, I would never vote again. I'm just not interested anymore.

What will happen if no one votes? If politics disappear? If the organization that shepherds society comes apart at the seams. On the flip side, what if everyone becomes zealots for their causes? Or if society polarizes into these two extremes. Politics are not a pleasure, they are a struggle. One of the keys to the system progressing and promoting quality of life is Balance. This comes through debate and compromise. We need active and well-rounded participants to represent different views - to work out the compromises and protect the innocent. The faction-forming potential for Assimilaire is grave, and whether the groups fall away in ambivalence or rally unto death it will be the undoing of nations and individuals will suffer.

"Yikes," was all Emmaline could say. She was aware that she had missed this point before because of her ambivalence to the system. She always believed in bringing about change through small actions in her own sphere. But she could see how that type of change requires generous spirit and co-operation. If it was met with concerted efforts to destroy the values being spread so slowly, the good would never have a chance to flourish. Hers was a philosophy born of relative peace and definite prosperity - a protected notion. What if the fabric of society frayed into loose threads and could not be rewoven? 'Yikes,' indeed.

Emmaline was about to close it up, but noticed an email came in from Ronny. Curiosity got the best of her. One more before sleep. What would a rocker/roadie write?

I just wanted to say that I'm not OK with this. It was fun at the conference, but ties choke me, and I swore I'd never wear one. What's my girlfriend gonna say? I feel like a geek on wheels, and it's even weirder that I like it. I hope this wears off soon. Can't see how this will make me fit in. I'm into Jade, and I don't want her to hate me. She'll think I'm a freak.

Emmaline's grim laugh punctuated her sleep-addled resolve. These letters along with some snippets she'd gleaned would have to be enough to get the point across to corporate. It was four, and she had only until eight to get enough rest to put her mind and will in strong order. Charlie's emails had stopped coming in by two-thirty. She decided to count on at least an hour when she arrived at work to get it all together and discuss it with Charlie. Surely they wouldn't call them in for a report until at least eleven, and if they were lucky, it might be after lunch.

She rummaged in her bag and found her toothbrush and paste, washed her face, grabbed a glass of water and set the dreaded alarm. She melted into the comfort of her own bed and managed not to dream about her presentation.

= TWENTY-SEVEN =

The alarm began to sing and Emmaline's creative consciousness molded the scene of her dreamscape into a concert. Then her body twitched awake, and she rolled enough to see the clock. It was daylight and eight-o-one, but to her rubber muscles it felt like a dark abyss where time was no more - if only.

She splashed through the downpour after leaving the bus, grateful for her boots. She focused on reaching the espresso stand. The young man who served her so many times before appeared as she rounded the corner. Emmaline held up three fingers, and he nodded with a toothy grin. Triple-shot cappuccino with her name on it - just a few more oar strokes ahead. She flashed him an equally toothy smile when he handed her the cuppa. She stopped to take an appreciative slurp before handing over the soggy money.

"I'm Emmaline," she said. "I've been buying coffee from you for a couple years and never asked your name." She wiped the back of her hand across a *blop* of water that splatted on her cheek from the awning's edge, and revealed her smile again.

"Gianpaolo," he replied with a bow-like nod. "My pleasure, Emmaline." His eyes shone a sparkling olive as he retreated further beneath the awning to get out of the squall.

"Have a great day, Gianpaolo!" she called as she also retreated, nearly running down the street through the deluge.

On the dot of ten she hauled off her boots and slipped on her girl-shoes, preparing for the big pitch. Charlie had been well-settled at his desk when she blustered in. She could have believed he'd been there since she'd left for the conference by the way he gelled with his surroundings.

"So are you ready for the big sell?" she asked him.

He flipped his cowlick with his palm and leaned back with an exaggerated leg stretch. "Well," he said at half the speed of her whole question, "I've been going over some more of these emails that came in after I went to bed last night. I've been here since eight-thirty."

"You came in early?" she grinned indulgently, easing into the well-worn groove of the familiar.

"Couldn't sleep. Hey, you know, Emmaline, this stuff is a lot creepier than I gave it credit for. I find it hard to believe they didn't get any inkling of this mind bending thing. I'm glad you and I didn't take the stuff."

"Ew, yeah, can you imagine if they made us take it as a tester in department meetings and we all became Arnies," she giggled, shivering off the last of the dampness from the Seattle November morning. "So let's get down to business."

She ran over the chosen pieces out loud with Charlie, and put them into a PowerPoint template as they went. He had also saved the voting one out of the batch. He thumbs-upped her inclusion of it.

"Anything else that is a must-present?" she asked him.

"Well, I really like the one from Mildred in Chicago. It just came in this morning."

She minimized the presentation and popped up her email. Emmaline was silent while she read the five line message. Charlie stared at her face like a dog watching a dangling sirloin.

"Augh!" she squealed and burst out laughing. "That's horrible!"

"It's great!" he snickered, his eyes sparkling in triumph.

"Yes, it's great," she agreed. "It's the coup de gras."

She jumped as the door to the Batcave swung open to the outside world.

"Good morning, Emmaleeeen!" Arnie enthused as he arrived.

"Hello, Arnie," she smiled through gritted teeth. She minimized her email.

"I hear the WWPA Con was quite a wingding."

"Sure was. Crazy stuff, Arnie you would've loved it," Charlie answered him and raised a surreptitious eyebrow at Emmaline.

"Great, great. I'm looking forward to hearing all about it at the meeting. You'll be ready by eleven?" he looked back and forth between them like one of those cat clocks with the tick-tock eyes.

Emmaline stole a look at her monitor. Ten till. "Yeah, we'll be there, just a couple more things to finish up." She reopened the PowerPoint and leaned into her monitor hoping for once he'd catch a clue.

"Oh, okay. Hard at work! That's my crack-shot team!" he cheered, and withdrew from the room.

"Whew!" Emmaline expressed.

"Go, Emmaline, go! Let those fingers fly!" Charlie encouraged in an Arnie-like tone.

She crushed twenty-minutes-worth of outlining and visual presentation creation into seven minutes and saved it onto a flash drive. After she ejected it she waggled it in front of Charlie's face. "Wish me luck!"

"Knock 'em dead," he wished.

=

Even Emmaline's nerve quavered when she came into the conference room and found not only Jensen, Product Development, Production reps and Joe, but Steve Schleagel, Marcus Wananabe, and Jennings Foreman - the big three. She calmed herself by embracing the fact that Schleagel-Martin was taking it as seriously as she was.

As Joe called the meeting to order, she flipped her eyes to Charlie hoping to gain support. He didn't return her glance, but it buoyed her up to watch him ambling to his position with his customary tall drink of water.

"The special presentation of *Assimilaire* at the WWPA Con in Chicago was a smashing success but developed some unexpected wrinkles," Joe began. "In the many tests and studies conducted before the drug's release, it was never conceived of to try the medication in a group setting where subjects took it at the same time, in the same environment. When this occurred at the conference kick-off, there seemed to be a type of mass bonding to our two models, Charlie and Emmaline. They became instant celebrities. By later that night, it was discovered they were not only being admired, but deeply emulated. We asked them to stay at the conference to study the phenomenon, and to prepare a report for us. Emmaline." He gestured her in.

"Good morning. Yes, as Joe said it was quite a ride! And as it turned out, not only did we get a chance to meet in classes with our emulators - or as we called them, 'Assimilairies' - but fate bottled us up in the hotel during a bomb scare and series of blasts." She swallowed her memories of the victims. "You have likely heard about it on the news. This intensive contact gave us more insight into *Assimilaire's* character in a couple days than we could've orchestrated in several months. It was a Godsend." She paused dramatically.

Joe cocked his head, perhaps unsure what was meant by this particular emphasis?

"What we found during this eerie journey was that *Assimilaire* worked in a different manner than we understood from the presentation given to us by Product Development. Instead of giving an individual a feeling of identification with a group, and bolstering their sense of self, it seemed to mold their psyche to the thought patterns and sensibilities of the models presented to them at the time of ingestion of the drug. Our assumption is that this was never noticed in study, because it took a large group taking the drug with only two models, to see the pattern emerge in a blatant way. And boy was it blatant!" She switched on the PowerPoint.

As Emmaline reviewed the events of the weekend - touching on the mob of adoring fans, the bar full of clones, the bursting-at-the-seams classes, the homogenous happenings in triage, and finally, the confessions at the fountain - she watched the faces of her audience change. Pride, intrigue, satisfaction, doubt, worry, and then a major split between purpose and defense. She plowed forward through the testimonials. Until she was interrupted.

"Sorry, Emmaline," Steve Schleagel from the Top office spoke firmly. "I just can't let you go on without comment. You've pointed out some incredible food for thought and study on what the brain response is to this pharmaceutical, and your anecdotes are fascinating. But you've moved on from observation to conspiracy theory. The only thing that's alarming here is that you discussed these wild conjectures with the public. You're in marketing. You should know such wild rumors can ruin our company's reputation. Don't you think it's a bit much to jump from people wearing similar clothing or noticing artwork to death gangs? We've gone from pseudo-Charlies to Charlie Mansons in one great leap."

"But these are not points we made up for presentation. These are actual reports from subjects who took *Assimilaire*, felt its effects and considered the consequences. I can give you a list of their email addresses if you'd like to ask them about it yourself," she retorted.

"They were under a great deal of stress, fear and fatigue. I think the dark hallways and threat of violence pushed you all to the edge of hysterical thinking."

"But what about what happened in triage? You could maybe discount the fact that so many women came to help. Even though I have cited testimony from several that it was against their nature. But what about the pseudo-Charlies fainting as they entered the door? There was no way for them to mimic or otherwise divine this reaction from Charlie or hysteria. It is a basic psychological reaction." She backed up the PowerPoint. "And this one's from an EMT."

The room was silent.

"Okay," Marcus responded, "I'm willing to concede this brings a different characteristic to the medication than we have considered up to this point. I think it would be irresponsible to ignore this new data and the breakthrough psychological influence it represents. The observations introduce the possibility of mind and behavioral control. It warrants further study. It may lead to other pharmaceutical breakthroughs and product releases for us. We could potentially change the face of modern psychiatry."

"The face of modern psychiatry? This may change the face of the earth," Emmaline was adamant. "How can we even think of further developments and releases when we should be recalling this one? We can't ignore the negative responses and possibilities and just move on."

"I thought that was where you were headed with this," Steve cut her off. "There's no way we're going to pull *Assimilaire* off the shelves, so you can give that up right now. The only ones who know of this interesting development are those of us in this room and a few traumatized individuals that were caught in a bombing zone. No one has been harmed. There is no FDA basis to force us off the market while we continue research."

"But what about moral basis?" Emmaline tried, becoming desperate.

"We haven't seen evidence of moral corruption," Steve stated.

"It can be clearly extrapolated from the type of psychological bending that occurred, that if the models were..." Emmaline continued.

"It is clear to you, but it warrants a lot more study in a scientific setting before any conclusions can be drawn," he interrupted.

"But who will you choose for the subjects of these studies...or the models? Are you going to model sociopaths? Would you take *Assimilaire* yourselves?" Emmaline exuded fire from her eyes, and Charlie's eyes flamed with fierce support.

"Actually," Steve said, "that's a great idea, Emmaline. We really can't know how mind bending it is until we've felt its effects. It seems the subjects from the conference went home with no more ill effects than too much desire to take it again. Let's give it a go. Production, do you have samples?"

Emmaline's mouth dropped open as a guy from Production dithered about trying to find enough product for them all close at hand. Her lips crimped in determination as her mind raced on how she could use the situation to clench the deal.

"So, do you want us to recreate the scene at the conference presentation?" she asked coyly.

"No, but you can continue your current presentation if you move away from your agenda to pull the product from the shelves and get back to anecdotes and hard observations. And since many of us are gentlemen in the room, how about if Charlie joins you to provide a model of his gender as well," Marcus directed.

Charlie rose from his seat without his usual ease, and joined Emmaline at the front. His expression told everyone he wished for this to be over.

Assimilaire dutifully swallowed, the assembly sat with unwavering attention ready for Emmaline to continue.

She retold the expression of Greta's day out on the streets of Chicago to give the women the joy of artistic resonance. Then she encouraged Charlie to recount one of the great conversations he had on music and the social significance of punk's individual expression to bring together future society. When she could see that the room was with them - moving to harmonize with their sensibilities - she went back to what she called, in a humorous tone, 'the Dark Side' of *Assimilaire*.

"And in closing I share with you an email, received this morning from Mildred in Chicago, which made my blood run cold." She put up the slide.

"She writes: *I took some* Assimilaire *at the conference and had a wonderful time. I attended the final meeting by the fountain with my friend Karen, but frankly didn't understand what all the fuss was about. When I got home that evening I took another dose that I had stashed in my notebook after your class. By bedtime I was petrified and slunk to my room in humiliated horror. I may not have noticed if I had been on my own, but with the introspection suggested by the fears of the others, I discovered a terrible nightmare... I had become my mother."*

A round of gasps and expressions of 'ew,' 'yikes,' and other such things escaped the women. The men lounged around the table smirking and shaking their heads, eyebrows cocked in mock disgust.

A blonde young woman came in from the reception area looking sheepish but urgent. She whispered to Joe, and he gave her the floor.

"Since this meeting is about the effects of *Assimilaire* in Chicago, um, we thought we should let you know right away. There's breaking news about a violent attack at one of the restaurants in SeaTac airport. It was done by people that got off a plane returning from Chicago this morning. We saw it on the news in the lunchroom…"

The conference room rose as one entity and moved toward the lounge area where there were a couple flat-screens. They assembled during the rundown of current weather and then latched on to the screen when the report began:

Earlier this morning, Mando's at SeaTac airport became a sea of mayhem as several passengers on flight 642 from Chicago to Seattle disembarked and walked into the popular coffee shop and stormed the kitchen, gaining access to knives and other utensils which they used to attack diners and workers.

The group from the meeting groaned and stood with furrowed brows to hear the rest.

Seven patrons were removed from the scene with stab wounds - two in critical condition.

The news cameras panned to shots of the blood-drenched pandemonium. All of the men from the board room abruptly fainted.

ABOUT THE AUTHOR

Sheri J. Kennedy is an individual who thrives on creating. She's a visual artist, photographer and writer. LIKENESS is her third novel. She studied philosophy, literature and communications which gave her a B.A. in Humanities. Thoughtful curiosity influences all of her pursuits. She enjoys participation in her community and life with her husband in a small house on the banks of the Snoqualmie River in the mountains near Seattle, Washington.

sherijkennedyriverside.wordpress.com

Photo Credit: Brenda Huckle, Genuine Image Photography

The Buzz from Readers of LIKENESS...

"energetic, fun language made for a quick, happy read. BONUS: i quite liked the concept!" dedmanshootn (aka dave walton), winner of *Most Books Read* in Bellingham Public Library's Summer Reading Program 2015.

"Emmaline is a strong business woman with fears I could totally relate to. I fell in love with her!" Sarah Salter, avid reader and contented barista

"Give me a good-sized dose, of Charlie! Line up the pseudo-Charlies - but none is as charming as the original. Lucky Emmaline!" Victoria Bastedo; author of ROOTS ENTWINE and DEAR MIKLOS

"LIKENESS is an interesting book and a great fiction read for the more philosophical or psychological leaning reader." Rachel Barnard, author of AT ONE'S BEAST

"Never before has the impending apocalyptic dystopia been such an amusing romp." T.A. Henry, author of SCRIPTING THE TRUTH

Other Books by this Author...

Free-Flowing Stories
from FreeValley Publishing
Sheri J. Kennedy, Editor
with Rachel Barnard & Kathleen Gabriel

An Anthology featuring eight Pacific NW authors from the Cascade foothills.
From spicy humor and savory storylines to luscious prose and sweet escapes, this banquet of literary treats is sure to whet your appetite for FVP's full course novels and to satisfy the bookish hunger of even the most voracious readers.

SECRET ORDER OF THE OVERWORLD
by Kennedy J. Quinn
(aka Sheri J. Kennedy)

Book One: UNDERNEATH & Book Two: OVERCAME, the complete series under this one cover.
A Lyrically written and Thought-provoking Fantasy Journey with Vivid, Morally Complex Characters in an Inspiring Story of Hope.

FIND OUT MORE ABOUT THESE AND OTHER GREAT
BOOKS AND AUTHORS
FREEVALLEYPUBLISHING.COM

FIND OUT MORE ABOUT SHERI J. KENNEDY &
KENNEDY J. QUINN
**SHERIJKENNEDYRIVERSIDE.WORDPRESS.COM
KENNEDYJQUINN ON FACEBOOK**

Made in the USA
San Bernardino, CA
08 October 2015